the
PRODIGAL
Heiress

a novel

the PRODIGAL Heiress

VICKEY ROGERS

TATE PUBLISHING & Enterprises

Published by Tate Publishing & Enterprises, LLC
127 E. Trade Center Terrace | Mustang, Oklahoma 73064 USA
1.888.361.9473 | www.tatepublishing.com

Tate Publishing is committed to excellence in the publishing industry. The company reflects the philosophy established by the founders, based on Psalm 68:11,
"The Lord gave the word and great was the company of those who published it."

Book design copyright © 2011 by Tate Publishing, LLC. All rights reserved.
Cover design by Kellie Southerland
Interior design by Chelsea Womble

Published in the United States of America

ISBN: 978-1-61739-671-7
1. Fiction, Christian, General
2. Fiction, Christian, Romance
11.02.18

This book is dedicated to my Lord and savior, Jesus Christ.

Acknowledgments

I want to thank the following people who helped shape the person I am and encourage me in my writing.

Those people are:

My dad, Marvin; he taught me that loved ones are not just blood relatives. He also taught me never to hesitate in helping others. My daughters, Tori and Susie; they taught me the joys of having children and now grandchildren in my life. My baby sister, Lauri, in whose eyes I am the person I wish I could be. Her faith in Jesus has always been an inspiration to me. My dear friends, Winnie, Marty, and Mike; who gave me the encouragement I needed.

Cynthia, a wonderful lady; she taught me that kids are important people too.

And last, but most certainly not least, Pastor Ungemach who not only took time out of his busy schedule to read my story, but also gave me feedback and encouragement.

I love you all.

Chapter 1

*L*exington Natalia Hunter was by no means skinny, but she had a trim figure that women envied. She considered herself of average height, neither tall nor short. When not tied up, her chestnut brown curls fell to her waist. She had a very pretty face and the greenest eyes anyone had ever seen.

Many men had fallen for Lexi, but not one had gotten her. Men would have only gotten in her way. She learned enough in college to know that. She would wait until she had everything she wanted, and then she would see if there was someone she wanted to spend time with.

At twenty-four she was serious about making her way in the concrete jungle and making a name for herself. Money was the real name of the game, and she wanted to win big.

She was starting out in an entry-level job, but she had already been noticed by several people in high positions who would be of help to her in the future.

Lexi sat down at the kitchen table in her tiny apartment to pay the bills that were due soonest. As she sorted the mail, a letter from an attorney in Washington came into view. Her heart beat a little faster. What would an attorney be writing to her for?

Nothing good, she thought.

She stared at the envelope a little longer and then tore the envelope open.

"I might as well get it over with," Lexi whispered.

Dear Ms. Hunter,

Please contact our firm as soon as possible. We have a matter of great urgency to discuss with you. We tried to get a phone number for you but have found you either do not possess one or your number is unlisted.

I must stress this is an urgent matter and of great importance to you. Please phone 1–888–555–2793 at your earliest convenience.

Sincerely,

Grover Sutton

Lexi eyed her cell phone while tapping the folded letter against her palm. She reached for her phone then pulled her hand away quickly. She felt like calling right away, and then she felt like waiting to see if it would just go away. Putting the letter up on the refrigerator, she decided to concentrate on paying her bills. She would get back to the letter later.

While Lexi wrote checks for two of the bills and paid the others online from her laptop, she kept glancing at the letter. It had way too much of her concentration. She had learned how to block out everything while learning what she needed to get the kind of job that paid the kind of money she wanted, but this was something she could not block out for some reason.

Finally, the bills were paid. Her shoulders slumped when she discovered that she only had fifty dollars left for the week. She had gone a little crazy shopping the week before and had to pay her credit card off with her paycheck. She always paid it off at the end of the month so she was not charged interest. She was good at watching money, just sometimes the clothing stores were too hard to resist. She did, however, always make sure she paid her bills before their due dates. Content with that thought, she turned back to the letter.

Lexi decided to get it over with and call the attorney. She picked up her cell phone and flipped it open. She dialed the number and listened to it ring five times before a machine picked up. She had forgotten it was Saturday, and the office was probably closed. She hung up, deciding to take a glass of wine into the bathroom and take a long hot bath.

She lit candles and put on some soothing Native American music, the slow rhythmic drum beat seemed to match her heart beat and the flute did wonders in lifting her spirits. Lowering herself into the steaming water stung but then felt heavenly. The sweet aroma of the bubble bath she had added to the steaming water transported her to a garden full of roses when she closed her eyes. She sipped her wine and let her mind wander.

As usual, her mind wandered to the future: a high-rise apartment in the rich part of town, a doorman to open the door for her, a man to operate the elevator—she wanted all of that. A chauffer, a limousine, and a bank account that seemed to bulge the walls of her financial institution; that was what she was willing to work very hard for as long as she had to. Anyone who got in her way wouldn't stay there for long.

She daydreamed that she was in a beautiful bathroom in a black marble Jacuzzi, fresh cut flowers all around her, twenty-four-karat-gold fixtures, and a breathtaking view of the city. Lexi smiled as the feeling of luxury calmed her and made her feel that indescribable feeling of pampering that she longed for.

Her daydream was cut short by her cell phone buzzing close to her head. She dried her hands quickly and picked it up. It was her mother. Lexi rolled her eyes.

"Hello," Lexi said irritably.

"Hi, dear…Your father and I were wondering if you'd like to come for dinner tonight. We're having chicken and rice."

"Mother, I haven't liked chicken and rice since I was ten. I prefer grown-up food now, steak or shrimp, or anything more elegant than chicken."

"Well, we can change the menu, but we haven't seen you in so long. We'd just love to see you. I also have something to talk to you about."

Great…More God talk, Lexi thought. She knew what this was all about. Her mother wanted her to go to church and do all the "good little girl" things she had forced her to do when she was younger.

"Mother, we've been over this a million times. I'm much too busy to go to church with you."

"Well, we'll see about that. I'm not giving up on that, but this is something else."

"What?"

"I want to speak to you in person."

"Okay." Lexi gave in, knowing she was not going to win this round. She would make a quick night of it pretending to have a bad headache. That one usually worked, although her mother would call for a day or two after, asking if she was sure she was all right.

Lexi lay back to enjoy her bath, but the mood was broken. She reluctantly got out of the bathtub and blew out all her candles.

"Dear, you look wonderful," Lexi's mother said as she walked into the kitchen. Miranda Hunter gave Lexi a tight embrace and was about to kiss her on the check.

"Hello, Mother," Lexi said stiffly. Her mother's kiss had not made contact before Lexi pulled away. She walked toward the sliding doors that opened to a small deck where her father was grilling.

"Well, we've changed dinner to be grilled steak with artichokes. How does that sound?"

"Very good, Mother," Lexi said, pleased with the change in menu. "So, what did you want to talk to me about?"

"Oh, well, let's go out to the patio with your father," Miranda said as she led the way through the sliding glass doors.

"Hi, baby." Frank Hunter greeted his daughter with a wave. "How do you like your steak?"

"Rare."

"Rare it is."

"Now, what is it you two want to talk to me about?" Lexi asked, a little irritated.

"Well, dear." Her mother paused and looked at her father.

"Baby, your great aunt, Camilla, passed away," her father said.

"Aunt Cami?"

Lexi felt a tug on her heart. Aunt Cami had been the one classy relative they had. She was the one Lexi wanted to be like. She owned a huge old mansion on the West Coast with a butler and chauffer, the whole nine yards. She was a snob to everyone except Lexi. She had found favor with her aunt and knew it was because they were kindred spirits. Now the only relative with class was gone, and she was left with these people who did not recognize the importance of money and stature and class. This was indeed a sad day.

Lexi was never really close to Aunt Cami. Her aunt had more important things to do than to play with children. She always sent wonderful, expensive gifts to Lexi on birthdays and at Christmas, things she did not truly appreciate until she was about twelve.

"That's too bad," Lexi said. "I liked her."

"The feeling was apparently mutual," said her father with a strange grin on his face.

Lexi looked quickly at her father, "What do you mean?"

"She left you everything," Lexi's father laughed and slapped his knee.

Lexi sat down hard on the edge of the table and stared at her father.

"Frank, that's a horrible way to tell her! You don't just blurt it out!" Her mother looked as if she were watching a tennis match. Her head kept going back and forth. Her expression was angry one minute, worried the next. Finally, the anger won.

Her mother railed at her father, but Lexi barely noticed. Her ears were ringing loudly, and her face felt flushed. She felt dizzy and nauseous.

Suddenly, her mother was there, supporting her.

"You see, Frank! You've shocked her!"

Her mother led her to one of the patio chairs, and she sat down heavily. Her mind was buzzing with a million questions and thoughts, none of which made any sense.

Only one thing stood out: Lexington Natalia Hunter was now an heiress, an heiress to a multi-million-dollar fortune, a mansion on the ocean, a yacht, a limousine—just so much luxury, far past her most cherished daydream.

"That must be what the attorney wanted. I'm supposed to contact him."

"Yes, dear…I had wanted to break it to you gently, but I guess your father was too excited."

"I'll need to fly out to Washington to see the lawyer, I suppose."

"I'll go with you if you'd like."

"No, Mother. That's all right. I can do this myself."

"You're so grownup. Okay."

"You coddle her too much, Miranda. She's a big girl now and needs to do things on her own," her father stated with a bit of an attitude.

When Lexi looked at him, her father winked. She gave him a thank-you smile and stood up.

"Would you both excuse me? I need to go home and pack."

"Oh, dear, but dinner's almost done. Stay and eat and then drive home. You're in shock, and you should really eat something. You're getting too thin," her mother coaxed.

"No, I, uh…I couldn't eat anything."

Lexi's stomach was in knots; but for the first time she could remember, they were good knots.

Chapter 2

The plane landed without incident early Monday morning. Lexi was beat. She had not slept for more than an hour at a time since finding out she was a rich woman. It was hard to eat and even harder to keep her mind on anything but how much her life had changed. She could not even daydream about the possibilities because they were endless. She had already sent notice to her job that she would not return. That would show them for not giving her a good position right out of college.

As she went to get her luggage, Lexi had to giggle softly to relieve the pressure in her chest from the urge to sing. She rubbed beside her mouth and smiled. Grabbing her luggage, she quickly made her way to hail a cab and gave the driver the attorney's address. Soon, she would be in the lap of luxury.

"Ms Hunter, please have a seat. Mr. Sutton will be with you shortly," an older woman who smelled of expensive perfume told Lexi.

Lexi sat in a leather chair that had to be one of the most comfortable chairs she had ever sat in. This attorney handled only millionaires and upper-crust people. It was obvious by his waiting room that he was favored by the wealthy.

"Ms. Hunter, you may go in now."

"Thank you," Lexi said as she walked with the air and purpose of a VIP. She kept her head up and pointed forward. She was walking the walk of confidence. Once she opened the door, her confidence faded for a moment as she peered inside the massive office of Grover Sutton. She suddenly felt very small. The fact that she was now an heiress came back to her, strengthening her.

Mr. Sutton had his chair turned away from her. As she closed the door, he turned around and stood up. A mop of gray hair with unruly curls and soft gray eyes that softened the starkness of his appearance put Lexi at ease. She felt comfortable walking up to him and taking his offered hand. Lexi craned her neck to look up at Mr. Sutton and smiled.

"Please have a seat, Ms. Hunter," Mr. Sutton said kindly. "I'm sorry for the circumstances that have brought you here today. Ms. Broadferd was one of my favorite clients. I share your grief deeply."

"Thank you. Aunt Cami was the only relative I felt I had a connection to. I'll miss her greatly." Lexi dabbed at a nonexistent tear.

"I'm sure, as we all will. Let's get started. I don't want to detain you longer than necessary. Your aunt was very generous with you. She left you everything. Now, while this might seem a blessing, it can also be a curse if you're not educated in handling this amount of wealth."

"I must admit I don't know where to start. Can you help me?" Lexi smiled at the attorney.

"Why, yes. As a matter of fact, I was going to suggest it. I was in your aunt's employ for thirty years, and I'd be pleased to help you also."

It was clear that he was very pleased not to have lost the account with the death of his client. Lexi understood that, even appreciated it. He was a man who knew the importance of people with money. She was now one of those people.

They talked about a few details, and then Mr. Sutton handed Lexi a very heavy ring of keys.

"These are to the house. Most every room locks, so that's why there are so many keys. Your aunt never updated the house. She only restored where needed. Will you be keeping the antiques, or will you be modernizing the house now? I can help you liquidate the antiques if that's your preference."

"I think I'll have a look at everything before I decide. It's been a very long time since I was there. It's all too gray a picture to make any decisions."

Mr. Sutton smiled, obviously pleased with her answer. True, most women her age were too foolish and naïve to realize the class of some antiques. However, she was not that foolish or naïve.

"Would you like to go out to the house now? I had Reeves, your aunt's...well now, I guess he's your... chauffer bring the car in case you wanted to stay at the house tonight," Mr. Sutton said. He smile and tilted his head slightly.

"Why, yes. I would love to." Lexi held back her excitement, not wanting to look like an overeager child. She knew her eyes were sparkling, but she couldn't help it.

"Excellent. I'll have him waiting in front of the building as you walk out."

"Thank you, Mr. Sutton. It was very good to meet you," Lexi said in a sincere tone, her eyes never leaving his.

He took her hand in both of his as she offered it and said, "I'm honored to have met you, Ms. Hunter. I trust you'll let me know if you have questions or if you're in need of my services."

"Yes. Thank you," She smiled sweetly, feeling like a princess.

Lexi headed out of his office and back toward the big, glass doors where she saw a large, black limousine waiting. A man of stocky build, medium height, and a pockmarked face stood ready to open the door.

She felt as if Christmas had come early this year, only no other Christmas could compare to this. It was her favorite holiday, all the rich colors and food and presents, especially from Aunt Cami. Now Aunt Cami had left her the greatest present she would ever receive: a mansion, cars, a yacht, and many millions of dollars to live the rest of her life in luxury.

Chapter 3

The drive to Rivenwood Manor was long, but the countryside was breathtaking. Lexi felt more at peace than she had in years. She would not have believed that being away from the lights and sounds of Chicago would be anything but boring. Somehow having attained her goal of wealth overnight had made her feel more at ease with the simpler life—or so she told herself. She had loved the hustle and bustle when she was trying to earn her fortune; but now that she had the wealth, who needed it? She would be happy being able to walk around her estate in the wee hours of the night and not have to worry about a strange person trying to rob her or any other horrible thing.

She would bathe herself in luxury and pamper herself totally. What more did she need? Her life was all she had ever wanted it to be now, and she was going to make the most of it.

Lexi drifted off to sleep, thinking of all the wonderful things she was going to do for herself. Thoughts of rooms full of roses and soft music, hours of relaxing, and hobbies born out of imagination and not necessity filled her dreams. She could do anything she wanted and go anywhere she wanted. Her life would indeed be full and satisfying now. Never again would she want for anything.

Lexi awoke as the car pulled to a stop in a circular drive in front of a beautiful, old, Victorian mansion. She was thrilled by the awesomeness of it. The chauffer hopped out and headed around to her door. She waited to move until he had opened her door and offered his hand to help her out. As she stepped out of the limousine, Lexi noticed the drive was made of huge stones that were relatively flat. How marvelous! She had only seen things like this in movies. She never dared dream her aunt's estate was this grand. Having been only three when she had visited, she did not really remember any of this. No wonder the few times Aunt Cami had visited she stayed at a hotel. Her parents' house was a hovel compared to this grand mansion.

The massive front doors opened, and a petite blonde in a maid's uniform came out to greet her.

"I'm sorry, miss. Tabitha's my name. The staff's off today. I stayed behind ta tend ta ya. I can give ya the grand tour or ya can look around at yer leisure. Miss Camilla left specific instructions for me, but I will do it yer way since ya are now the lady of the house," Tabitha said with a pleasant accent.

Lexi immediately liked her.

"Why, thank you for your thoughtfulness, Tabitha. I think we'll get along well."

"Yes, miss. I can take ya to the master suite and ya can start from there if ya'd like."

"That sounds fine."

Tabitha grabbed a suitcase and told Reeves to bring up the rest.

Lexi followed Tabitha into the foyer, which was bigger than her parents' entire house. To think she had always thought her parents had done okay for themselves.

There was black and white marbled, square flooring. The walls were made of dark green marble and dark cherry wood. A beautiful cherry wood staircase, a grand staircase indeed, sat in the middle of the foyer. It was at least twenty feet wide at the very bottom, narrowing to perhaps fifteen feet wide as it went up to an open hall on both sides. The halls led to the east and the west wings of the house. Lexi could have stood there all day and stared at its magnificence, but she did not want Tabitha to think she was out of her element. She wanted her servants to know that she was in a position of authority right from the start. She quickly followed Tabitha with her head held high.

Tabitha headed down the west wing. The halls were as wide as the living room in her apartment. There were tables and chairs made of antique cherry wood going down both sides of the hall under antique paintings of presumably ancient relatives. This place was too awesome to even register in her mind.

There were many doors, all huge and made of brilliantly shined, dark wood. There seemed to be a preference of dark cherry wood in the choices. It was breathtaking.

Tabitha stopped at the only set of double doors on the west wing. She opened both doors into the huge master suite. Lexi knew the minute she stepped in that the suite had not been used in many years.

"Wasn't this my aunt's suite?"

"Oh yes, years ago. Miss Camilla got too weak to ascend the stair case about five years ago. So she had a room made up for herself down by our quarters. That way we could get to her right away if need be. She had a stroke, don't ya know, and never regained her strength."

"I had no idea. I wonder why she didn't let anyone know."

"No. Not Miss Camilla. She never wanted help from anyone. She was a strong woman inside, even if her body didn't agree."

"But five years of not being able to see everything in her own home?"

"Yes, it did pain her, but she made sure that every inch of the house was properly cared for, including the attic. Not one cobweb up there, miss." Tabitha smiled proudly.

"Wonderful," Lexi said with a bit less enthusiasm. She felt oddly saddened thinking of her aunt unable to roam freely around this wonderful estate. "Can I see her room?" Lexi asked.

"Why sure. It is yer home, miss. Everything's open to ya now."

Lexi followed the maid to the first floor and then down a much less luxurious hallway that held the kitchen and all the servants' quarters. At the end of the long hall was a simple, oak door.

Tabitha took out a huge ring of keys identical to the one Mr. Sutton had given Lexi and unlocked the door. She then opened the door and stood aside for Lexi to enter. It was a single room about the size of Lexi's bedroom in her old apartment. There was a small TV, a twin bed with a simple white coverlet, and a small table next to the bed made of unfinished pine. There was a plain, gold-colored lamp with a white shade and a large-print Bible.

The floor had green-and-white tiles like the floor in her grade school had been. The walls were pale beige. There was a single window with pale green curtains. There was nothing fancy or luxurious about this room. It was a travesty that her aunt had spent the last five years of her life living like this in a mansion so full of beauty.

"Why was my aunt made to endure this cave of a room?" Lexi asked with unbridled anger.

"Now, miss, don't be upset. 'Tis as the mistress wanted. She said she had lived a life others only dream of, and she wanted to know how the others lived. She became quite earthy after the stroke. Think she might have wanted to prepare to meet her maker, I'd say."

"That's an awful thing to say. Being rich is not a sin," Lexi faced Tabitha with clenched fists.

"Din't say it was. I'm sorry, miss. I'm only tellin' ya how it was. The mistress wanted things this way. The mistress always got what she wanted. Always…" Tabitha said softly, visibly shaken at Lexi's hostility.

"Well, I wouldn't have put up with it if I had been here. She owned all of this and should have enjoyed it 'till the very end," Lexi let go of her anger slowly with a long sigh.

"Yes, miss." Tabitha avoided Lexi's eyes, keeping hers glued to her shoes.

Lexi began to feel guilty for dampening the girl's bright personality. She decided she had made her point.

"I want this room redone as soon as possible. Make it into a lounge for the staff. Anything you want in here is fine, just no smoking in the house. I can't breathe smoke," she said waiting for Tabitha to look her in the eye.

"Why, yes. I will tend to it tomorrow." Tabitha was visibly pleased. She smiled at Lexi and nodded.

"Make sure you get my approval on all purchases. I do want to be kept informed about my home."

"Yes, miss." Lexi heard the excitement in Tabitha's voice and felt better about the situation.

"Where are my aunt's personal belongings," Lexi asked as she again surveyed the bare room.

"She donated them all to charity. It was a final request," Tabitha said softly once again. Lexi know she was afraid of making her angry again. Then she realized what Tabitha had said.

It was odd. Lexi really wondered about that. Charities were all scams. She was sure of it. The people working for them took all the good stuff, she was sure. Her aunt must have known this, also. She was a shrewd woman.

Lexi picked up the Bible, knowing she might not find any other personal items of her great aunt's.

Lexi was getting tired of the girl. She must have been a few years older than Lexi, but she seemed younger, far younger. She seemed to have such a positive attitude all the time. How could anyone have that?

But then again, why was she in such a dour mood? She had every reason in the world to be happy, and she was feeling angry and a little depressed. It was strange. It must just be that she cared a lot more for her aunt than she had realized. After all, she was a very caring and thoughtful person. Yes, it must be the thought of pour Aunt Camilla stuck in that tiny hole for five years. That was it.

Once Lexi was back up in her suite, she found that her bags had been emptied and put into a small closet by the door. Someone had unpacked for her. She could get very used to this.

There was a massive clock hanging on the wall that looked almost like a grandfather clock but not as deep that said it was 5:30 p.m. She wondered when dinnertime was. There was a small box on the wall she thought might be an intercom. Lexi pressed the button.

"Yes, miss?"

"I was wondering about dinner."

"Oh, yes. I'm preparing it now. I'll get your preferences at your convenience. Mistress Camilla preferred dinner at seven sharp."

"That will be fine. I'm going to take a bath."

"Yes, miss. Fresh towels are in the bath."

Lexi walked over to another set of double doors and found the bedroom. A massive canopy bed with a deep purple velvet comforter beckoned. She might have succumbed if it was not for the appeal of a bath. She was sure it would be the grandest bathroom she had ever seen. There were two sets of double doors leading from the bedroom. The first she tried were to a huge, walk-in closet that was bigger than her aunt's room downstairs. Her robe was the only thing hung up in this closet. If her entire wardrobe was in this closet, it would look like leftovers after someone had moved out. She definitely needed to go shopping.

Lexi undressed and put her clothes into a large, wicker hamper and then pulled her fluffy robe from the hanger and tied it around herself. She then walked to the other set of massive doors opposite the closet doors. Beyond the doors was a world beyond her comprehension. There were many plants within the room. Some even had flowers in bloom. The two outside walls were made entirely of glass so she could see the ocean on one side and the mountains on another. It was amazing. It looked more like an area where you would have a gathering or special social event, not a bathroom. The tub was the size of a small adult swimming pool. There was an area to lay on that was padded inside the pool. This was a paradise.

Lexi turned on the water, which poured quickly from a waterfall across one entire end. She made sure the temperature was just right and then looked around the room a little more while the pool filled. She couldn't think of it as a tub. It just was not one.

Going over to the sink, she saw that it was free-standing since the wall was made of glass. There was more than ample room to see out, so she was sure the glass was the kind that could not be seen through from the outside. Not that it mattered a great deal with the ocean on one side and mountains on the other. She could see for many miles out over the ocean. It was fairly calm today, and the sun shone on the water as it was heading down for the evening.

She walked over to the other wall and saw the majesty of the mountains. A feeling of being a tiny speck came to her as she gazed at the beauty in front of her. The mountains had a rainbow of purple, orange, black, and silver from the late afternoon sun. It was so beautiful.

Turning back to the pool, she saw that it was almost filled. She took off her robe and draped it over a chair against the wall. She then walked down the little staircase that made entering the pool safe. The water felt very good. The water was very soft, not the hard water of her apartment. It felt heavenly.

The heat started to relax muscles she had not realized were tense. She did a short swim to get to the padding and noticed the shampoo, conditioner, and little rose soaps that were on the marble ledge. They were all very expensive, and the smell from the rose soaps was like sitting next to a bouquet of roses. She smiled at the luxury of it all. She shampooed her hair and put the conditioner in it and then used the rose soap to wash. She sat on the padding so she could lift her legs and feet out of the water to wash them. Then she dove under the water to rinse off.

Getting back up on the padding, she knew she would easily fall asleep. It was perfect, just like everything else in this house. She leaned back and took a deep breath. The water covered the padding and Lexi, except for her head, where the padding had a soft, pillow-like feel. The water totally relaxed her.

Sometime later, she was awakened by a humming noise. She looked at the wall clock to see that it was 6:45 p.m. The water was exactly the same temperature as when she had first gotten in. She then realized the humming was coming from a water heater of some sort.

Lexi pushed the drain button and climbed out of the pool. She dried off and wrapped her robe around herself. She walked out into the sitting room and to the small closet to dress for dinner. She chose a light brown, expensive-looking dress to dine in. She would be the only one at dinner, but it would be served to her.

Once she was dressed, she descended the staircase like a queen, feeling every bit as if she was one. At the bottom of the staircase, she realized she was not sure where the dining room was. She knew it must be on the east wing, near the kitchen. She started in the direction and was met by Tabitha.

"Glory! I was just about to come fer ya."

Lexi followed her to another massive room that held a huge, mahogany table with matching chairs, buffet, and sideboard. A huge fireplace sat at the head end of the table, and a small blaze was glowing cheerily.

"The mistress always loved a fire to dine by. I thought ya may like it after yer bath."

"How lovely, Tabitha. Thank you."

The maid beamed. She left and came back with a tray of very delicious-looking food. Lexi ate with a ravenousness she did not feel until the first morsel hit her tongue. She would have to make sure the cook knew about carbohydrates and how she wanted the food prepared from now on. She did not want to gain a lot of weight. For tonight, this was just what she needed.

The next morning, late morning, Lexi woke up feeling as if she had never slept before in her life. The bed was so soft that she felt as if she was floating; and the room was very quiet, no cars honking or people yelling and making all kinds of noise. When the lights were turned off, you could not see your hand right in front of your face. It was divine. Even though it was a tiny bit scary, she knew she would get used to it.

So began her first real day as mistress of the house. What should she do first? She supposed she would need to meet the staff and go from there. They should be back today. She dressed in a formal suit that showed her authority the best and put her hair into a tight bun. She wanted to look professional, in charge of the situation, and command their respect.

As Lexi descended the staircase, a young boy ran through the foyer, dragging a kite behind him.

Lexi became very angry. Where had a child come from? She did not want children in her home. They were messy and never listened to a word you said. They caused all kinds of problems. She descended a little faster until she was at the bottom. There was a buzzer on the wall that she assumed was a call button. She was right. Once she pressed it, a man she presumed must be the butler was at her side almost instantly.

"Yes, miss?"

"I want to meet the staff."

"Very good, miss."

The man left; and within minutes, all her staff was lined up, ready to greet their new mistress.

Tabitha did the introductions.

"This is Raymond, the butler," she said about the tall, thin, gray-haired man with the deep voice who had gone to get everyone.

"This is Chris. He is the cook and the best one I have ever known," she said of a young man with a red face and almost-white hair.

"And this is Burdia. She oversees all of us and makes sure we are doing our jobs," she said of a tall, thin woman about her mother's age. She had a stern-looking face—piercing, gray eyes; a stark, birdlike nose; and very thin lips. The woman had a look of curiosity on her face, but Lexi could tell the woman had a dislike for her that was not going to sit well. She would see about getting a new overseer or whatever she was.

"Fine…Whose child was that I saw running across the foyer a moment ago?"

"Sorry, miss. That was my nephew. Mistress Camilla let me bring him with me when my sister has her doctor appointments."

"I'm not my aunt. I don't like children, and I don't want the boy here after today. He may remain for today."

The sparkle in Tabitha's eyes dulled dramatically. "Yes, miss."

Lexi immediately regretted her words. She should have talked to Tabitha alone, but she could not take it back now, not with all the staff watching. They would think her a pushover and she had to let them know that she was their boss. Well, no matter. She was sure Tabitha's sister could find a sitter. Aunt Camilla had just been too generous in her old age. Lexi would need to remind all the staff that they were servants, not houseguests.

It was strange, but for some reason, that rationale did not make Lexi feel much better. She would have a talk with Tabitha later when the others were not around. Then Tabitha could reassure her that she was in the right so she would not have to feel this way too long.

Once the servants had departed to their tasks, Lexi summoned Raymond to have Reeves pull the car around. She was going to spend the first day as mistress of this house spending some of her money. After all, she needed to fill that closet upstairs.

That evening, she came home exhausted. She had spent $20,000 on new clothes and really did not have that much—no where near enough to fill the closet, but she was content. She bought a few other odds and ends and spent well over $5,000 for them—beautiful candles for her bath, a bottle of very expensive champagne and a set of twenty-four-karat-gold-rimmed wine glasses. She had also dined in a very posh restaurant, which alone had cost $250, but what was that to her millions? No need to worry about how much things cost anymore. She had an endless bank account.

Lexi directed Raymond to bring her things up to her room and leave them. Once they were all there, she closed the door to her suite and took the candles into the bathroom and arranged them perfectly. She filled the pool and lit all the candles. She took one of the wine glasses and opened her champagne. Filling the glass, she then placed it by the padding in the pool and went to her closet to get her robe. She placed her clothes in the hamper and donned her fluffy robe. She walked back to the sitting room and grabbed the box of imported chocolates that she had bought at the same shop she had found the glasses and champagne at. Then she went back to the pool.

She slipped into the water, washed up, and then relaxed on the padding. She sipped her wine and ate the chocolates until she was satisfied. What a life. She was so very happy with this life. She needed nothing else.

Suddenly, she noticed what looked like a panel that could be removed from the ledge of the pool. She tried to open it but had no luck until she pushed down on it. It then rose up; and she saw it was a lighting, stereo, and TV-control system. A panel in the ceiling opened, and a huge screen slowly lowered into view when she pushed the TV button. When she pressed it again, it retracted into the ceiling.

She pushed the lighting button and found that the lights could get very bright or so dim you almost did not know they were on. The stereo had all kinds of luscious classical music.

"Aunt Cami, we had so much in common. I wish I had known you better," Lexi said softly.

Lexi felt much better after her bath. She dressed and summoned Tabitha to her suite. She sat in a high-backed, cushioned chair that was comfortable but felt like a throne. She put a short-backed, cushion-free, straight chair across a small table from her chair and motioned for Tabitha to be seated when she arrived. Tabitha took the chair, acting quite meek. Not her usual manner, Lexi noted.

"Tabitha, I wanted to talk to you about your nephew."

"I promise he will never come with me again. I need this job, miss. I support not only myself but my sister and nephew," Tabitha pleaded. Her eyes were frightened.

Lexi felt even worse than she had earlier.

"Why can't your sister afford to take care of herself and her child?"

"She has cancer. She's been fightin' for three years now. She can't work. She keeps Demetri at home with her except when she has to go in for a treatment. But we have arranged with the hospital to take care of Demetri when my sister goes in."

"How are you able to pay for her care?"

"Your aunt was very fond of Abbey and Demetri. She provided for them in life and in her will. But there are other things besides her treatment that I pay for."

Lexi was shocked she had not learned of this before. Well, they had made arrangements with the hospital; so she need not feel guilty for not wanting the boy here. She made up her mind that all was fine, even though there was a nagging doubt at the back of her mind. She pushed the thought away and stood. Tabitha stood also.

"Okay. Well then, everything is settled."

"Does this mean I still have my job?"

"Of course…Did you think I was going to fire you?"

"I should have asked about Demetri instead of springing him on ya. It never occurred to me that ya wouldn't like children."

"I don't like the messes children make. As long as they stay in their place, they're fine. I just don't want them in my space. That's all." Lexi smiled, hoping to ease the tension.

Tabitha looked doubtful but smiled slightly back. "Will you be wanting a late dinner?"

"No thank you, Tabitha. I dined out."

"Very well…Will ya be needin' anything else?" Tabitha asked in a very professional way that did not suit her personality.

"No thank you, Tabitha. I'll be retiring shortly. I have a big day planned tomorrow. I want to start inspecting my home and making some upgrades. Most everything is wonderful as is, but I noticed a few things I want to replace. I'll need your help tomorrow."

"Well, that would be Burdia. She is the overseer and—."

"No. I'm letting Burdia go. You will take over as overseer if you want the position."

"Are you sure about this? Burdia was with your aunt for the last thirty years. I have only been here five. I might not be a good choice."

"You'll do fine. There will most likely be a raise in your salary."

Tabitha look surprised. She truly wasn't thinking of a raise with a new position. She looked very unsure, as if she did not believe it. Lexi had not planned any of this. It was like someone else was talking through her. She did not like to see Tabitha so distant. She was the closest thing Lexi had to a friend here, and she did not want to alienate her. She also felt the voice in the back of her head quiet, which was good. She did not want Burdia here anymore either. So it was out with the old, in with the new. Everything would work out fine—or so she thought.

The next morning, Lexi went through the house with Tabitha in tow. Tabitha made notes of the changes Lexi wanted to make. There were not a lot of them, but one was substantial. She wanted to take down a wall in the main great room to open it up for a larger sunroom. The two rooms were already spacious, but she really didn't care for the somewhat dark great room.

Once she had an idea of what she wanted and had Tabitha document it all, she was on her way to summon Reeves to take her to town to do some shopping. Before she could get to the intercom, Burdia stepped in front of her.

"Miss, I hear you are looking to change some things in this house. I am the overseer, and I tend to all of these things."

Lexi was shocked at the way Burdia seemed to think she had any power over her at all.

"Excuse me, Burdia, but I need to summon Reeves to take me to town. It is no longer your business what I do with my house. I am relieving you of your position. I just need to talk to Mr. Sutton to find out what all I'm required to do by law."

Burdia sniffed at her and then grinned. "We will see about that, Miss Hunter. We will see."

Burdia turned and walked away with her nose in the air as if she was so much better than Lexi. Lexi was very angry now. Lexi's fists were balled so tightly her knuckles turned white, and her hands hurt. She stomped to the intercom and hit the button. She called Reeves and had him drive her into the city and to Mr. Sutton's office.

Lexi burst in on Mr. Sutton and another client, ignoring the protests of his secretary.

"I'm very sorry to interrupt, but I must speak to you at once."

"Certainly," Mr. Sutton said with a bit of confusion and irritation in his voice—not much, but enough to let his other client know he was just as annoyed.

Mr. Sutton took Lexi into a side room and motioned for her to sit on a very expensive-looking couch.

Lexi explained her problem with Burdia and asked Mr. Sutton to draw up a legal form and severance package so that everything would be legal.

"I'm terribly sorry, Miss Hunter. I should have explained more to you, but time was not on my side. Burdia Wiffles was left her position in your aunt's will. It was Camilla's way of rewarding Ms. Wiffles for all her years of faithful service."

Lexi was beside herself with rage. "You mean I'm stuck with that woman?"

"I'm afraid so. But let me assure you, Ms. Wiffles is an excellent overseer. She has kept things going smoothly at Rivenwood Manor for some thirty years. She is very good at her job."

"But she treats me as if I'm beneath her. And I have made plans to change a few things, one large thing, take out the wall between the sun room and sitting room, and—."

"I'm sorry?"

"The great room is so dark. I feel taking that wall out will provide much more light."

"My dear, you're allowed to change everything but the structure of the house. You may add rooms and walls, but nothing may be torn down."

"Wait. I thought this house belongs to me."

"It does, with certain stipulations. I'll have a copy of the will sent to Rivenwood Manor by currier later today. I'm very sorry. I hadn't realized the problems a delay would cause. The copy of the will explains everything."

Mr. Sutton got up and offered her his hand. Lexi got up slowly, took his hand, and then walked back out to the limousine in silence.

The drive back to Rivenwood Manor seemed much shorter than the trip into the city. Lexi was not looking forward to seeing Burdia's face. She knew the woman would be gloating.

Lexi managed to escape Burdia as she entered the house. She went up to her room to wait for the copy of the will. What other nasty surprises were there that Aunt Cami had decided to burden her with, she wondered. Her paradise had lost some of its wonderfulness. She almost felt like she was a trapped animal. Well, not quite. She did not have to live here, but how could she not? The bathroom was like heaven on its own. Maybe she could live with that dower-faced, old woman as long as she did not have to come into much contact with her.

There was a knock at the door. Lexi got up and opened it to Burdia.

"So, you found out that you can't replace me. Now, about those changes…Let's start with the wall," she said as she walked past Lexi and into her suite.

"Mr. Sutton told me all about it and is sending a copy of the will. I'd appreciate your not coming in without invitation, Burdia. Whatever my aunt left you, she didn't leave you the right to invade my privacy."

Burdia sniffed and turned to walk out the door with her head up.

"Burdia, if you keep that attitude, I'll move to some other house, take the staff, and let you rattle around in this house all alone."

Burdia's head whipped around, and she stared at Lexi. Lexi had struck a nerve. Burdia hadn't thought she would move out or take all the other servants with her.

"Miss, do you know what this house is worth?"

"I'm sure I can't even imagine. But I won't be treated this way by a servant. You might have been close to my aunt, but I am now the mistress of this grand manor, and I expect the respect that goes along with it."

"Very well, but just remember I know how to run this house. I know all its secrets."

Burdia turned and left. Lexi wondered what she meant by secrets and decided that Burdia was just trying to annoy her. She turned back into her room after closing the door and her gaze fell on her aunt's Bible. She became curious. Had her aunt written anything in it? Were there any clues as to why she would leave this all to Lexi and then put down impossible stipulations? Hmm, she wondered.

Lexi picked up the Bible and sat in the high-backed chair. She slowly turned the worn pages as she skimmed the text. She noticed that many pages had highlighted sentences and paragraphs. She wondered if her aunt had become senile or if maybe she did it as a sort of game.

Lexi read some of the highlighted markings and saw things she had heard her mother quote at times. She also remembered a few from Sunday school when she was young. It was very odd. Why had Aunt Cami wasted time highlighting things in a Bible? Sure, it was a nice book that held a lot of good advice for life; but why would anyone mess around more than to leaf through it? Well, she was an old woman and probably bored.

The word rang in Lexi's head. Come to think of it, she was kind of bored now. She decided to take a bath. She had a few more bottles of that wonderful champagne and some of the chocolates left. A little pampering sounded like just the thing to change her mood.

Later that day, the will arrived. Lexi was thankful there were not too many more bad surprises. She had to put up with Burdia, she could not change the existing structure of the house except to add on, and she had to make sure all the staff was provided for for the rest of their lives. A waste of money, she thought; but she could not change the will, so she would go along. She had gotten a lot in return for these pains. She could live with them, she decided.

Chapter 4

The next couple of days turned into a couple of weeks and then into a couple of months. Time seemed to move slowly, one day melting into the next. One day, a letter arrived from Lexi's mother. She really had no interest in reading the letter, so she went to take her bath before dinner.

When she finished her bath, the letter seemed to be calling for her attention; so she opened it and read it.

Dearest Lexi,

Hello, sweetie. Your father and I hope you are doing well. We tried to call but could not get a number, so I decided to write to you.

Honey, I hate to tell you this with you being so far away, but your father is ill. He is not in the hospital or anything like that, but he is not going to be able to work for quite some time, so he's at home. I know if you could call and say hi to him it would make him feel a lot better. He misses you very much, as do I.

He is very depressed now and knows the company won't hold his position for the length of time his doctor says he will most likely be off.

How are things out on the West Coast? It must be beautiful this time of year. I always wanted to live on the west coast, but your father's work kept us here. Now would be a perfect time for us to visit you because your father's not working, but at the same time we have to watch every cent. Funny how life works sometimes, huh?

I know you are very busy taking care of all the things I am sure need your attention with all the responsibilities that you have inherited, but if you could please call or write us dear and let us know how you are doing. We miss you greatly.

Love always,

Mama and Daddy

Lexi was aggravated with the letter. She knew she should probably feel bad that her father was ill, but her mother said things in such a way that she did not want to contact them at all. Lexi certainly did not want them coming to visit. It was nice not having her mother call every couple days to see if she was still alive, as if she could not take care of herself. She decided to send a telegram. She summoned Tabitha and told her to send a telegram to her parents. The telegram would say, "Hope you feel better soon, Dad. I'm fine but very busy. Love, Lexi."

Tabitha gave her an odd look.

"Is something wrong?"

"No, miss. I, uh…"

"What is it?"

"Your parents…your father is ill?"

"Yes."

"I'm sorry, miss." Tabitha turned and left.

Lexi knew there was more that Tabitha wanted to say, and she knew it would have angered her; but at least she had the sense not to say more.

More time drifted by, and it was now November; and the weather was getting dreadful. The slight boredom Lexi felt shortly after her arrival at Rivenwood Manor was starting to become more pronounced. She had so much and was already tired of it, tired of the baths and relaxing. She was even bored with spending money. She did not think that was possible, but she could not think of anything she wanted that she had not already bought. It was unreal to her.

The fancy lunches she had at fancy restaurants were just not that fun by herself. Spending money on clothes only the staff saw left her feeling lonely and took the fun out of it. Having all this money and no one to be envious was flat and unexciting.

She decided that she needed to make some friends. As much as she did not really care for people, she realized that they were a necessary distraction. Not only that, but she could also show them how classy she was. What good was all this wealth and luxury if there was no one to notice? The problem now was how and where could she make friends? She had a few acquaintances in college and at work, but where would she go to meet people of her stature? She decided to talk to Mr. Sutton. He should be able to give her a few ideas, and she knew he would keep it confidential.

So the next morning, she set out for the city, this time waiting until Mr. Sutton was free.

"Miss Hunter, what a nice surprise." Mr. Sutton smiled.

He seemed much happier to see her this time than the last. She was relieved since the matter she had to talk to him about was fairly embarrassing.

"Hello, Mr. Sutton. Thank you for seeing me without an appointment."

"It's always a pleasure."

Mr. Sutton directed Lexi to take a seat in the chair across his desk, and then he sat in his own chair. "How may I be of service?"

"Well, I have a bit of a problem. I know it might not be the usual thing a lawyer helps a person with, but I don't know anyone else to talk to."

Mr. Sutton watched her intently. He seemed very interested in her problem. This made Lexi more comfortable and at the same time a little more embarrassed to ask. She knew of no one else, and she could not bear being in that house much longer with no changes.

"I worked very hard through high school so that I could attend college on scholarship. What my scholarship did not pay for, I worked to cover."

"Yes. Your aunt told me quite a bit about you. She admired you greatly."

"I never knew."

"Yes. She was looking for an heir, and I would say she couldn't have chosen better."

"I wish I could have known her better." Lexi was silent for a moment and then decided to just get the question out. "Mr. Sutton, I have no old friends or new ones. I'm going insane with boredom and need some relief. Where could someone like me go to make suitable friends?"

Mr. Sutton seemed bothered by her question. "Suitable?"

"You know, I can't go to regular clubs. People would want to be my friend just to try to get at my money."

"Ah. I see. Well, have you thought of renting a cottage on the beach? People wouldn't know of your wealth if you were to have a place to entertain that was nice but not too nice."

"Well, I would like to show off the house. I mean, I would love to entertain there."

"I see. You could join the Brighton Hills Country Club. There you would be able to meet others of your stature, although most of them are a bit older than you. Their children would be close to your age. I'm not sure they frequent the club though."

"Well, that sounds like a beginning anyway. Thank you, Mr. Sutton."

Mr. Sutton gave her a card and told her to let the club's staff know that he referred her for membership. He would fax over a written recommendation in the morning. Lexi thanked him again and headed back to Rivenwood Manor.

The next morning, Lexi dressed in one of her most corporate-type suits and had Reeves take her to Brighton Hills Country Club. She had called them and made an appointment for an interview. A woman named Mrs. Stratford had said that Mr. Sutton's letter had already arrived, and they would be honored to see her at 10:00 a.m. She assured Lexi that the interview was just a formality that would be over in moments and Lexi would be welcomed into their close-knit family. Money talks, Lexi thought.

When she arrived at the club, Lexi was awed by the beauty of the place. Even in the dreary, rainy, dim light of the day, it was breathtaking.

The driveway and parking areas were made of dark red brick. Instead of curbs, there were neatly sculptured bushes, so dark green they were almost black.

The club itself was the same dark red brick but with gold brick trim. There were so many windows and gables that the building would have looked like a gothic mansion, except for the golden light within that gave a warm, inviting glow.

Over the huge entrance was a large stained glass window showing a beautiful rose bud. The light behind the window showed it off perfectly.

A doorman ran out from the entrance and held a very large umbrella that shielded Lexi from the rain as Reeves opened the door for her and helped her out. Lexi smiled at the attention. It made her feel good.

The building was as impressive, if not more impressive, on the inside as the outside. There were lush, green plants everywhere; a lot of dark, mahogany wood; white marble with silver threading; and deep red, leather chairs and couches.

A woman holding a folder rushed to greet her.

"Miss Hunter, I'm so happy to meet you. I'm Marylis Stratford. We spoke on the phone."

"Hello Mrs. Stratford. Please call me Lexi. It's a pleasure to make your acquaintance." Lexi smiled warmly.

"Please call me Marylis, Lexi." She smiled warmly in return.

She ushered Lexi into a large office. Lexi sat down on a settee, and Marylis sat down next to her. She was a thin, frail-looking woman probably in her sixties. She had thinning, blonde hair coiled in a tight bun. She had almost an old-time school teacher look to her. Lexi wondered what type of person she was.

"Now then…Just fill out these forms, and I'll enter the information into our computer and you'll have all membership rights. We have an indoor, Olympic-sized pool, a large health spa and gym, gaming rooms, party rooms, a movie theater stocked with all the most current movies, and that's just for the cold weather months. During summer, we have trails and outdoor swimming and cabins and, well, here is a pamphlet that lists all the amenities. This is a place where you can come and do anything. I wish more of our young people would take advantage of this place rather than the city club circuit. It's so destructive. I'm sure once they find out about you; more will want to spend time here. They're always interested in new people who are worthy of their company."

Lexi smiled. She then filled out the forms and handed them back to Marylis. Once she had entered all the information, she took Lexi on a tour. Each room proved to be more impressive than the last until Lexi felt that this club was almost as impressive as her home. She wasn't sure how she felt about that, but Rivenwood Manor was still more impressive.

Marylis gave her a key and told her the club was open twenty-four hours a day, seven days a week to her, holidays included. It was like a second home. Lexi felt very comfortable with the atmosphere. She would definitely use the club a lot and make some new friends.

"You have special privileges here, my dear. If Mr. Sutton didn't tell you, your aunt was and actually still is one of our biggest benefactresses. She left a large amount for maintenance of the buildings and grounds that will last for many, many years. She also bought all the plants you see. She had a passion for plants."

"Yes. I can tell. My home is full of them." Lexi smiled.

"Okay. Go ahead and make yourself at home. Go and enjoy anything you want. This is your place now. You can live it up, relax, or wait around. It starts to hop a bit around here at the dinner hour. We have a world-renowned chef working here. There are also some very nice apartments on the west wing. Your key fits L234. It's on the main floor. You have French doors leading out into the rose garden. It's very beautiful in the summer. The apartment is yours to use or not as you please. It's cleaned daily whether or not you use it. If you want privacy, there's a red satin ribbon you tie on the knocker. You'll be left alone until the ribbon is removed."

"This is all very impressive."

Marylis beamed. "So glad you approve. I'll see you later, Lexi." She took Lexi's hand and then gave her an impulsive, quick hug. "I know you'll love it here." And with that, she was gone.

Lexi explored, met a few older couples, and finally checked out L234. It was a quaint apartment, very nice and richly furnished but a bit on the small side. The thought immediately struck her as funny. She giggled quietly. Four of her old apartments would fit into this one. Well, her life was much grander now than it had been then. It was another lifetime.

She walked into the kitchen and found that there was a menu lying by a house phone. She was a bit hungry and ordered herself a lunch she wouldn't soon forget. It was absolutely the best food she had ever tasted. The dinner roll was brushed with a mixture of olive oil and garlic. The marinara sauce on the pasta had so many distinct flavors that all came together perfectly and made Lexi's mouth water as she lifted each bite to her mouth.

She walked over to the French doors after lunch and looked out at the garden. There were a few roses left; but even without the full blooms, it was a magical garden. There were trails and stone benches and beautiful, full trees. Beautiful statues were placed perfectly to enhance the majesty of the garden. She could not wait for summer.

She decided to see what movies were playing. She did not know what was out in the theaters. Television was something she never turned on anymore except for the news. She saw that there was a movie about two college friends who ended up dating the same girl that started in fifteen minutes. It sounded all right, although romantic comedies were not her greatest interest. She preferred real-life dramas about the wealthy. She did like to watch old war movies at times, which she could only associate to her growing up watching them with her dad.

A pang of guilt hit her. She had not gotten in touch with her parents to see how her father was doing. She had been so busy trying to cure her boredom. Well, she would call him soon and see how he was.

She opened the door and found a very large theater, just like the public ones, only with seats that were so padded she knew if the movie was boring she would fall asleep. The floor was polished marble and was immaculately clean. To one side of the staircase which led up the rows of seats was a small booth where you could push a button and fresh, hot, buttery popcorn was dispensed. Next to that was an ice and pop dispenser with clear blue plastic cups. This place really did pamper its members.

Lexi sat on the very top row in the middle. She wondered if they played movies even if no one was there since it looked as though she would be the only one there for the movie.

Lexi was surprised to find a handle on the side of her chair that brought up a foot rest. This place was like a huge home, and she felt more pampered than ever.

About two minutes before the movie started, a group of people walked in. Lexi slid down a little so they would not see her until she wanted them to. They were younger people, about her age. She sat up a bit, and the five people saw her.

"Hey up there. You don't look familiar," a very tall, professional-looking young man said in a deep voice. He smiled to show that it was his way of greeting her.

Lexi got up and walked down the staircase to where three young women and two young men stood watching her.

"Hello. I joined the club today. My name is Lexi Hunter."

One of the women gasped. "Camilla's niece?" she asked with an astonished look on her face.

"Why, yes. You knew my aunt?"

"Hardly…She never came around here, but she is the talk of this club. We had heard you were a recluse."

"Dotty," the young man with the deep voice admonished her, "is that the way to treat a new friend?"

"Well, darling, it's just what I've heard." Dotty leaned up against him and practically purred. She was tall and thin with glossy, black, shoulder-length hair, black eyes, and the exotic beauty of a black panther.

"Lexi, don't mind Dotty. She has no manners. I'm Jeff Gary." He held his hand out to her, which she took and shook firmly.

"This is Appel Broughter," he gestured at a tall, somewhat chubby young woman with short, curly, blond hair and sparkling, blue eyes.

"Glad to meet ya, Lex."

Lexi shook hands with Appel and liked her immediately.

"Here we have Houston Cheyenne," who was about six feet tall with a trim, fit build. His arms looked like he was a body builder. He was dark and very good-looking but seemed very unfriendly also. He did not offer his hand but stood there, looking her over. She felt extremely uncomfortable with his gaze.

"And this is Lark Winston," he gestured to a willowy, mousy, brown-haired young woman. She smiled faintly and shook Lexi's hand.

"Very pleased to meet you, Lexi," said Lark with a bit of bored sarcasm.

"Well, that's our little group. Shall we all have a seat and enjoy this miserable show?" Jeff asked lightly.

They all sat down. Jeff made sure he sat next to Lexi, which she could tell Dotty did not like at all. She practically sat on Jeff's lap, which Lexi thought was funny. The last thing she wanted was a relationship with a man, especially someone else's.

The movie was a little better than Lexi had anticipated, and she even laughed out loud with the others a couple of times. Jeff kept patting her hand and asking if she "heard that." She knew it was a habit of his by the way he kept doing it, but it made her feel like a fifth wheel. Dotty gave her a scathing glare more than once.

When the movie was over, they all got to their feet.

"Well, Lexi, got any plans for this evening?" Jeff asked.

Lexi saw a murderous look on Dotty's face but knew she would have to get over this hurtle sooner or later if she wanted to have friends.

"No. Not really. I was just going to stick around here and see what came up."

"Awesome. We're going to a party at my cousin's house. She throws the wildest parties around," Jeff said with a wink as he took Lexi's hand and put it on his arm.

"Am I dressed appropriately?"

"You look divine. You'll fit right in," said Appel. "By the end of the party, you might have nothing on, so it really doesn't matter." She laughed loudly, and the others joined in.

Lexi stopped walking for a moment, causing Jeff to look at her questioningly. She was not into that kind of lifestyle. Then again, she had been cooped up in the house for so long and had missed her college experience to put herself through college. She needed to be less frumpy and have some fun, she decided. She shrugged, smile at Jeff, and they continued on their way to the party.

Fun turned out to be a lot more than Lexi had bargained for. The evening started off nice. She met a lot more people whose names she promptly forgot after each introduction. She was given a glass of a delicious wine, and there was beautiful music playing in the back ground but not too loudly.

Jeff's cousin, Trina, was as tall as Jeff and very beautiful. Honey-blonde hair coiled around her head, and she had the bluest eyes Lexi had ever seen. She took an instant liking to Lexi and kept her near her for hours. Lexi learned that most of the people at this party had grown up together. She heard a lot of the wild pranks they had pulled on family, teachers, and even each other.

A tray was brought out. It contained white powder that Lexi knew must be cocaine. She passed, but not without a lot of urging. Finally, the others gave up, and they all started doing lines. Lexi was disgusted with the habit, but she did not let it show. These were her friends now, her only friends; and she would have to make allowances. They were also in her class, so who was she to judge?

The music got louder and faster, cigarette smoke filled the rooms, and alcohol and cocaine were being served continuously by waiters. Lexi kept drinking the wonderful wine, but it seemed to have a bit of a kick to it. She was starting to feel very funny. She had never gotten drunk, and she was only sipping this wine very slowly; so it surprised her that she suddenly needed to sit down. She found a spot on a white leather couch and set her drink on a coaster. The room started spinning.

She looked up and saw her only anchor, Trina, toss her keys to Jeff and yell, "I'm leaving with Brad. Go ahead and lock up after everyone goes home." And she was gone. Lexi wanted to call out to her but instead leaned back and closed her eyes. She had no strength, no energy at all.

Sometime later, she awoke to blearing music, laughter, and a hand on her arm. It was Appel.

"Hey Sweetie…Ya passed out. How much of that firewater did you have?"

"I think about four glasses."

"Oh my gosh Honey! There's straight grain alcohol mixed into that fruit juice. Goes down smooth. But oh, you're goin' ta hurt in the mornin.'" Appel helped Lexi to her feet.

"Come on, hon. You come sit in the hot tub with me. Maybe we can sweat some of that alcohol out of you."

They went out past the pool that was loaded with inebriated people and walked down a path leading to a large, brick building. Lexi realized that it was raining very hard and wondered at the people in the pool. It was also fairly chilly, but she supposed they had not noticed, given their state. She had just realized that she was soaked to the skin herself.

They walked into a large room filled with rose bushes and the largest hot tub Lexi had ever seen. She had no idea that anything that big existed. Appel flipped a switch, and what looked like candles turned out to be little gas flames that gave the appearance and feel of hundreds of candles lighting the room. It was magical. Appel stripped off all her clothes and got into the water.

"Come on, Lex. It's wonderful."

"Are there any suits here?"

"Oh, come on. It's just us."

Lexi, being less inhibited than normal and certainly not in the best frame of mind to make decisions, took off her clothes and hung them on some branches to dry and then awkwardly climbed into the tub. It felt so warm and relaxing. She found a seat and leaned her head back. She was almost asleep when something brushed lightly on her neck. She opened her eyes to find Jeff smiling sleepily at her. She sat up quickly and realized she was clutching a sheet to her tightly. She was in a bed.

"How did I get here?" she squeaked.

"You don't remember? You and Appel were in the hot tub, and I happened to come in. You called me over, started kissing me, and, well, one thing led to another. We decided to come up here for some privacy."

Lexi blushed deeply. She did not want this.

"Did we…?"

"Well, I would love to say yes, but we both passed out," he said regretfully.

Lexi felt an immense relief. This was one problem she didn't need or want.

"Where are my clothes?"

"I would think they're wherever you took them off," he said as he jumped out of bed and got dressed. "Do you remember where that was?"

"By the hot tub. I can't believe all this."

"It happens." And he was gone.

She wondered, had anyone else seen her naked? Did she just walk up here with nothing on? She felt huge waves of embarrassment and humiliation run through every inch of her body. She had a very fit body, but she definitely didn't want to parade it around for the world to see.

About ten minutes later, Jeff returned with her clothes, which were dry.

She felt too embarrassed to ask but too afraid not to ask. The fear won out.

"Jeff, did I walk past people with nothing on?"

"Sure, but not that any of them noticed. The only one who was in any shape to notice would have been Houston, but he had to leave to attend some family thing. Go ahead now. Get dressed."

He left the room to give her privacy. She was very relieved that he was a gentleman when he was sober at least.

When she was dressed, Lexi searched for the kitchen. The house was big but nothing like Rivenwood Manor. She found Jeff pouring two cups of coffee.

"Thank you, Jeff. I really feel foolish for everything. Thank you for being such a gentleman."

"Lexi, I consider you a friend. Yes, we just met, but I would like to continue our friendship. And if it turns into more than that…I would rather it happen because we both want it to, not because we couldn't control ourselves."

Lexi was amazed at his honesty. She smiled at him.

"You do amaze me."

Jeff smiled warmly. "How would you like some eggs and croissants with your coffee?"

Lexi's stomach flip-flopped. "No, thank you."

Jeff chuckled. "Sorry. I had to tease. Anyway, I have a meeting this morning. You can lounge around here. Trina likes you, so it would be okay. Or I can call your man to come and get you."

"Yes. I should get home. There are a few things I need to take care of today."

Jeff called for Reeves to pick Lexi up; and then, as he was leaving, he planted a sweet kiss on her cheek. Lexi had never met a man like Jeff. Then again, all the ones she had known were all boys—poor boys at that.

Chapter 5

*S*oon it became normal for Lexi to go out every night with her new friends. She became more and more like them. She had never experienced this kind of life before; and it was, in a way, freeing. They laughed at the way they woke up feeling like death warmed over and the periods of time they could not account for. They also relayed tales to each other of finding themselves in the oddest places when they awoke. Oddly enough, Lexi always woke at home in her own bed. She could never remember what had happened past a certain point.

She had started smoking also, but only when she drank. Mornings were always bad, a hangover and lungs that felt like they were on fire. By 5:00 p.m., when she would take a bath and get ready to go out, she felt much better.

Houston started to warm up to her. He still never really smiled, but he was now in a habit of helping her out of the car and opening doors for her. She was in a habit of teasing him about his quietness and making him smirk ever so slightly. She knew he loved the attention. She even became bold enough one night to kiss him soundly on the mouth as they celebrated a day without rain.

Houston seemed to be watching over her, which Lexi found comforting in a way since she never awoke in public places the way Dotty did. Nor did she end up in bed with anyone after that first night with Jeff, when she could not remember what happened. She thought maybe he was protecting her from herself. She also never saw her photos or stories about her wildness in any of the tabloids. She knew Houston had a big part in that, as his father was one of the main owners of those tabloids. He had good connections. She also never saw Houston take a drink and wondered why he was with this crowd, but they accepted him the way he was, and so did she. She went on with her friends and lived a different life than she had ever dreamed of.

In this new world of hers, she found that every day had something in it they could celebrate: no rain, someone getting a new car, someone buying a new house, or updating a wardrobe that hadn't been updated in the last few months. Lexi realized there was always a reason to party. She found the little voice inside her was getting smaller and softer. It was the one that kept telling her she was doing very bad things and would regret them. After the first couple of times that she awoke feeling ashamed, a few laughs with the others made the shame dim dramatically.

The partying continued, and Lexi lost more and more of her inhibitions. She even won Dotty over by giving her meaningless compliments in public, which she found was something the very shallow girl ate up. Lark was no one's friend, but she accepted Lexi as much as anyone else. Appel and Lexi became like sisters, but they spent all their time together drinking. No real connections were made, which at times bothered Lexi; but she accepted things for how they were. It was better than the boredom she had felt in the fall.

It kept her not so much happy as occupied her time. It totally obliterated the boredom.

One morning, Tabitha knocked on her door. It was almost noon. Lexi was upset because she had a very bad hangover.

"Come in," Lexi said, lying on her stomach with her arm hanging over the side of the bed.

Tabitha opened the door and poked her head in. When she saw Lexi looking at her with blood shot eyes, she walked in a little further.

"Miss, did you want lunch," Tabitha asked softly.

"No. Why are you bothering me with this," Lexi asked, rolled her eyes, and turned her face away.

"We are worried about ya, miss. We don't see much of ya, and ya seem to be always under the weather," Tabitha said quickly and held her breath as she wrung her hands.

"I'm fine, Tabby. Just sowing my wild oats…I never got a chance to do that before. So please leave me alone." Lexi appreciated but felt overly annoyed that Tabitha had come to her room.

Tabitha kept her distance after that.

One day blurred into the next. She vaguely remembered a Christmas tree, the noise and kisses of New Year's, and then Jeff got all the girls large boxes of chocolate for Valentine's Day. The Fourth of July was spent on Jeff's parents' yacht, partying hard and throwing up over the side.

The next thing Lexi knew, she was laughing and drinking spiked cider on a Halloween hayride. She and the group laughed at all the disgusted looks they got from people with kids who all decided to wait for the next wagon instead of getting on with the inebriated group.

Time was flying by at a tremendous speed. Lexi spent her time either drunk or sleeping off the alcohol. A few times, she felt scared at the way her life was flying by and how she was not actually in control of things; then she would think of her friends and somehow felt safe in their company.

Then she saw the Christmas tree in Appel's house and realized that over a year had gone by since she met this group of people, and she felt sick and oblivious to the world around her. It frightened her more than she had ever been frightened before. She decided to talk to Appel about it.

"Appel, do you ever feel afraid? I mean, time seems to have sped up so fast. I've known you guys for over a year now, but we don't really ever talk. We just drink and joke around. It's already Christmas again. I feel like I have totally lost touch with the world and normalcy."

"Nah…What else is there but boredom? All the bad things that happen in this world, I would rather be disconnected from this miserable place. You're just being silly."

"You really think it's better to go through life numb?"

"Of course I do. Nothing can hurt you when you're numb." Appel laughed and grabbed a bottle of bourbon. She took a long swig and handed it to Lexi.

Lexi took the bottle and stared at it.

"Come on, Lex. Don't start getting all thoughtful. You'll ruin a great party. Dotty has a band flying in tonight. We can dance to a real band. Now that'll be loads of fun."

"You're right. Why spend the evening being depressed when I can have a good time?"

"Exactly!"

So Lexi worked hard to forget the fear and just go along with her friends.

Lexi fell into a kind of hibernation, not caring about anything and feeling content to feel that way—until the news of her father's death shattered her contentment in early August. In her quest for relief from her boredom, she had forgotten to inquire of his health. She had also not bothered to read the growing stack of letters from her mother until Mr. Sutton called to inform her of her father's passing.

Now she sat down to read them and found that her mother had frantically begged her to come for a visit, that her father missed her terribly. She also found that her mother had been trying to beg her for help. They needed money for treatments that might have saved her father. Lexi had been too busy trying not to be bored, trying to be happy. When she really thought about it, she had not been happy. She had been numb.

Now it all crashed in on her. She had never seen herself as a selfish person, but now her selfishness had caused her father's death. He had died without knowing his daughter, his only child, had still loved him.

If only she had read those letters. She could have made a difference. She knew it. She was too busy drinking under a tree in the Goshmeir's orchard or cleaning vomit up off the floor of whoever's house she had gotten sick at. She felt such shame and loathing that she could not stand it. She needed to get to her mother right away. Oh how her mother must hate her, and with good reason.

Lexi sent a telegram that she would be arriving that afternoon. She tried calling, but the phone had been disconnected.

Chapter 6

he flight seemed to take forever. Once the plane landed, Lexi took a cab to her parent's house. She gave the man a large tip and jumped out and ran to the house. She opened the door and found that her parent's house was very sparsely furnished. What had happened to all the antiques her father loved so much?

"Mom," Lexi called. "Mom, where are you?"

A neighbor woman came around the corner from the kitchen.

"Well, if it isn't Miss Too-good-for-her-own-family." The woman seemed to look at Lexi from the end of her nose.

"Mrs. Witherby, I know I have been horrible. But I need to see my mom right now."

"Oh, you need to see her, huh? What about when they needed you?"

"Gale, please." Miranda Hunter hugged and then stepped around Mrs. Witherby.

Lexi was shocked at the thin frame that glided toward her and hugged her. Lexi hugged her mother back and felt as if she were hugging a sickly thin child. She was bone thin. She must have gone through hell. Lexi's eyes welled up with unshed tears, tears she would have cried for herself but hated herself too much to do so. Now they came freely for her poor mother and father, the people who took care of her as she grew up, the people who made sure she had everything she needed. She had been so blind with the lust for money. She realized she had blamed her parents for not being rich. How could she have been so hateful?

The realization was a shock. Maybe these were things she had always known, but never had she given them room to grow until she received the news of her father passing away.

"Oh Mama…I am so sorry for what I have done."

"Dear, you haven't done anything."

"Exactly…I was so busy playing that I didn't have time to read your letters. If I had, Daddy would still be alive."

Miranda led Lexi to a ratty couch. The beautiful antique with dark red, velvet covering and dark, shiny mahogany, sculpted wood was gone. They sat down, and Lexi cried harder.

"I am so ashamed, Mama. Please forgive me for how horribly I have treated you."

"Lexi, you're human. Don't beat yourself up or try to blame yourself for this. You were given something that was much too big for you to handle, and it drew all your attention. It would've happened to anyone. You're not alone in that. And your father has gone to heaven because that's where he's supposed to be. He's not gone from us forever, you know. He has just gone home, and we will join him one day. Please, baby, don't blame yourself. It's how it's supposed to be. I fought to keep Daddy here with me, but God wanted him. It was his time, and I know that now. It's something you need to accept also."

"But if I had read your letters I could have done something."

"No. If God had wanted Daddy here now, he would have put an urge in you so strong to read those letters that you couldn't have resisted."

Lexi looked at her mother with wonder. She loved what she saw: a brave, beautiful woman who loved and trusted God more than her own life. Lexi felt she was seeing her mother, truly seeing her, for the very first time.

"Mama, I'm so sorry for how selfish I've been. I've spent two years drunk with people I barely know. I've lived so foolishly, so stupidly. I want to make it up to you, but I also want to make it up to Daddy. And it's too late for that." Lexi sobbed even harder.

"Honey, Daddy always wanted you to be happy and have everything you needed. He was so happy for you. You need to remember that your happiness made your father happy. And the drinking, well, it obviously didn't make you happy. But it's never too late to change your life."

"But I should've brought you both with me. I could've afforded to get Daddy the best possible care."

"Lexi, honey, you're going in circles. You need to forgive yourself for this and realize that God just wanted Daddy with him."

Lexi realized she was making her mother console her when she should be the one consoling her mother.

"Okay. I'm all right. How are you doing?"

"Well, I have good days and bad days, but that's the grieving process. I spend a lot of time with Jesus, and that makes me feel a lot better. And I know your father is in a good place now. No more pain and he can never get sick again. So I'm just dealing with missing him."

"And the huge bills that are left behind," Mrs. Witherby exclaimed, giving Lexi a hard glare.

"They will all be paid in full tomorrow. And, Mama, I want you to come and live with me. We'll bring Daddy to Washington and have him put to rest in the family plot on the manor grounds."

Miranda looked at Lexi. There was such astonishment in her eyes that Lexi felt even more ashamed.

"That's very sweet of you, honey, but—."

"No buts, Mama. I'm doing too late what I should've done to begin with. So you go and start packing everything, and I'll make all the arrangements."

Miranda stood up and looked as though she would faint.

"Are you okay, Mama?"

"Yes. I, uh…I…guess I better start packing," Miranda said in amazement and went to her bedroom.

"Fine how you can do so much now. You ought to be ashamed of yourself, missy."

"Believe me, Mrs. Witherby, I am more ashamed of myself than your tongue-lashing will ever make me feel," Lexi said as she brushed past an astonished Mrs. Witherby, who had never been the kind of person anyone ever talked harshly to. Lexi was on a mission for the first time in her life. She was thinking of someone other than herself for once. It was not just to ease her guilty conscious, she realized. She really did want to make her mother's life better. Her mother deserved it.

Lexi made all the arrangements, asking for constant approval from Miranda; and soon, they were on their way to Rivenwood Manor. Lexi held Miranda's hand as they took off, since Miranda has never been on a plane before, and she was very nervous. Lexi teased her and made her feel more comfortable. She was actually enjoying herself. This was something she never felt with any of her friends. With them, it was all going along to get rid of boredom. With Miranda, it was easy and fun and no pressure. All this time, she had this wonderful woman she could have been close to, but she had to wait until she appreciated her. It was all making sense now. Her life had brought her to this point. She was very glad she was finally here. At the same time, she was immensely saddened by the fact that her father was not with them to enjoy it.

Lexi decided she wanted to help more people, and she decided that the next people would be Tabitha's sister and her nephew. She did not really like the idea of having a kid running around the manor; but if Tabitha kept him under control, she would be all right with having the boy there. Her mother might like having a young child around sometimes. Miranda loved children.

Chapter 7

*L*exi got a thrill out of showing Miranda Rivenwood Manor. Miranda was like a child, wide-eyed and ooing and ahhing at all the right places that made Lexi feel that she was giving her mother a present.

Lexi gave her mother the master suite and took a less grand but just as beautiful suite down the hall. Miranda protested that she did not need anything so big, but Lexi would not take no for an answer. Miranda sensed that Lexi needed for her to take it, so she finally gave in.

"Mother, look at the size of this tub," Lexi said as she led Miranda into the bathroom. Miranda stopped short when the tub came into view.

"It's not a tub. That's a swimming pool," Miranda said and laughed whole heartedly.

"I have an idea. Do you have a suit?" Lexi asked with a gleam in her eye. She was almost dancing with the idea that was forming in her head. Her feet would not stay still.

"No," Miranda said as a smile slowly spread to her eyes.

"It's all right. I have one that should fit you. Let's get in," Lexi said as she ran to get the suits.

Both put on suits and got into the very warm pool. Lexi turned on some music, and they relaxed for a while.

"This is wonderful, Lexi."

"I wish I had brought you and Daddy here with me right away," Lexi said with a sad voice.

"Honey, like I said, things always happen for a reason and in the way they are supposed to."

"But doesn't that make God bad in some way?"

"Only to people who don't know him. He has a plan for everything. There's nothing that he doesn't have control of."

Lexi marveled at her mother's faith. She had seen Miranda break down in tears again and again at the loss of her husband, but she kept saying that it was because she missed him. It was the pain of her own grief, not any grief for Lexi's father. He was in a much better place. She kept saying this so often that Lexi started to believe her.

"Mom, Tabitha has a nephew. He's about four years old. Would you mind if he spent some time at the house?"

Miranda looked up at Lexi with eyes that were full of questions. "Honey, this is your house, not mine."

"This is our house, Mom. What's mine is yours, just like you told me when I was growing up. So again, would you mind?"

"Of course not, dear. You know that I love children. I didn't think you really cared for them being around though."

"Mama, a lot of the things I like and dislike are changing. I mean, kids have never been my favorite people, even when I was one myself. I haven't been around them much in a very long time, and I feel I need to make some drastic changes in my life. I feel like there's some purpose behind my life that I'm not aware of. I want to find out what it is, but I can't do that without testing things."

"Well, you're right about that. Oh, honey, I'm very excited. When is the little one coming?"

"I need to talk to Tabitha about it. Then I'll let you know."

Miranda had a sparkle in her eyes that Lexi had not seen since her father was alive. She knew this was a step in the right direction. She could feel it, and her heart was growing warmer and more content.

The next morning, Lexi called Tabitha into the study.

"Yes, miss?"

"Have a seat Tabitha." Lexi gestured to a high-backed, deeply padded chair that was very comfortable to sit in. It was much nicer than the hard chair she had offered Tabitha in her suite what seemed a lifetime ago.

Tabitha looked at her again to make sure she understood Lexi.

Lexi again gestured and said, "Please."

Tabitha sat in the chair.

"Tabitha, I'm not proud of the way I've been acting for quite some time. I've been cruel, insensitive, and boorish. I want to change, and I need your help, starting with your nephew."

Tabitha watched Lexi's face intensely. She knew that something was going to change, and seemingly for the good.

"I would like your sister and her son, if she feels comfortable with the idea, to move into the cottage on the grounds. We'll take her son in when she needs to see the doctor."

"Miss, are ya sure about this?"

"Yes. I have so much and nothing worthwhile to do with it. The cottage is so beautiful but has no one living in it. Your sister and her son can live there for nothing. Tabitha, I've come to the realization that my true friends are those around me, those who take care of me and are so loyal to me. The people I've been associating with are lonely, lost souls who are pulling each other down. We were drowning in our own desperation. I can't live like that anymore. I want a real life where I can help people who need help, not spoiled brats who can never get enough."

"Mistress Camilla said this would happen." Tabitha's face darkened with a blush.

"What else did my auntie say?"

"I can't say anymore. But she knew ya were a good soul. That's why she gave ya everything. She started to realize why God had given her all this, but the time had not come. It's you who will do what yer aunt started. I really can tell ya no more. But I know she was very wise in choosing ya."

"Thank you, Tabitha."

Lexi smiled at her, and Tabitha breathed a visual sigh of relief.

"Please make all the arrangements for your sister's move today, if that is acceptable. I also want to make available to her all the best doctors and treatments for her condition. I have so much money I can't spend it all in my lifetime, so whatever she needs, it's a gift from Aunt Camilla, all right?"

"Yer a good soul, miss." Tabitha jumped up and hugged Lexi tightly. "I knew it too. I saw it in yer eyes."

"One thing, Tabitha."

"Yes, miss?"

"What are your sister and her son's names? It's been a while, and I want to make sure I can let my mother know who will be joining us."

Tabitha laughed. "Sorry, miss. Abbey and Demetri."

"Well, let's get Abbey and Demetri here ASAP."

Tabitha ran happily from the room to get started on the day. Lexi found Miranda sitting in the sunroom, finishing up her breakfast of grapefruit and toast.

"Tabitha's sister and her son will be moving into the cottage sometime very soon, if it's all right with her sister. Their names are Abbey and Demetri."

"Wonderful."

Miranda looked very happy. It burned into Lexi's heart. Her mother was becoming her best friend. She knew this even though she had never had a best friend or a real friend at all. She knew that no matter how many people would now enter her life; her mother would always be the most special.

"Mama, I love to see you smile," Lexi said as she took Miranda's hand and kissed it.

"And I love to see you smile," Miranda said as she squeezed Lexi's hand.

"It's funny how different I'm feeling. I've never felt excited to get up in the morning except for my first day of work. That went away quickly. But I somehow know that from now on, every day is going to feel like this, a day I can't wait to start."

"That's wonderful, my sweet Lexi. It's what I have always prayed for you."

Lexi got up and kissed her mother's cheek.

Chapter 8

*L*exi's life became better than anything she had ever dreamed of. She no longer cared about showing off or how much money she had. She lived every day to see Miranda happy. It healed her guilt, and yet that wasn't why she was doing it. She found that her mother was a very inspiring person and so very generous. Growing up, Lexi had thought her mother was wasteful when she dropped money in the poor box at church and when she gave money she had intended for new furniture to the family down the street whose house had caught fire. Now she saw her mother in a different light. Her mother was someone to be looked up to, someone to strive to be like, not embarrassed of or avoided.

She was now able to talk frankly and openly with Miranda about the past and her feelings now. Miranda never hesitated to remind Lexi that she should not be so hard on herself, that she was growing as a person. Miranda tried to get Lexi to go to church with her, but that was just not something Lexi was quite ready for yet.

"One of these days, I might surprise you. But, Mama, I just don't feel any urge to go; but maybe one of these days."

Miranda looked at her daughter with a wistful look in her eyes, and yet the determination underneath was evident to Lexi. She smiled at her mother's strength.

The fall breeze was starting to become brisk when Lexi started to think about her friends. Houston and Appel were the only ones from her old circle of friends she was actually starting to miss. She decided to call and invite them to lunch. She was unable to get a hold of Appel, but Houston said he would come.

He arrived at exactly noon. He brought a bouquet of long-stem roses and a bottle of sparkling apple cider. Lexi thanked him and had Tabitha put the roses in water and serve the cider with lunch.

"Thank you so much for coming, Houston."

Houston nodded.

They walked to the back of the house to the sunroom, which overlooked the ocean. The day was sunny and a bit chilly but not too chilly to sit outside on the patio.

Lexi motioned for Houston to have a seat at an eloquently set table.

"Lexi, this house is beautiful," Houston said as he looked around. It was more than he had ever said to her.

Lexi's heart beat a little faster at the sound of his voice. She had never realized how deep and rich his voice was.

"Thank you, Houston. I love this house," Lexi said and smiled. Her eyes met Houston's and locked for a second before they both looked away shyly.

"You have never had the group over for parties. I see why now," Houston said knowingly.

"Yes. I couldn't have this beauty trashed," Lexi said, nodding her head. "Or find passed out people draped over the stone wall…" This time when their eyes met, they both smiled and shared a small laugh at their pasts, which alleviated a lot of their shyness.

"That's very smart," Houston said. Lexi realized he wasn't just good looking, Houston was devastatingly handsome. His white teeth were the perfect contrast to his honey colored skin. For the first time, she realized his eyes were not brown, but a deep, dark green.

They had a delicious lunch of lobster tails, a Caesar salad, and hot rolls that were Chris's specialty. It was a very satisfying lunch, and the sips of cider went well with the food. Lexi had gotten up her courage by the end of lunch to speak frankly with Houston.

"Houston, I asked you here because I've missed you."

Houston looked at her, his face showing he was surprised at her words.

"When my father died, it brought a lot of things into perspective for me. That kind of life isn't really any kind of life. It's more hiding than anything."

"You're right about that," Houston said, looking out at the ocean. Lexi could see his jaw working as he ground his teeth.

"But, Houston, you don't belong with those people. You're not like them. Why do you hang with them," Lexi said, taking Houston's hands in hers. Houston looked at Lexi, and she saw his eyes start to water.

"Because they're the only ones around who would give me a chance," he said looking deeply into her eyes. Lexi could see a lot of pain in his eyes.

"I don't understand," she said as she leaned towards him. Houston gently took his hands from Lexi's, got up, and turned away from her to the three-foot stone wall with the ocean view. He looked out at the ocean as he told her what caused his deep pain.

"When I was twelve, I took my father's car without permission. I was very wild in those days. I took it and went joy-riding with four of my friends. We had brought along some beer. I didn't know how to drive very well, and drinking didn't help. But I managed to get fifty miles from home before I lost control and killed my four friends."

"Houston!" Lexi stood and grabbed his arm.

He looked back at Lexi quickly, tears of pain filling his eyes.

"Do you want me to leave now?"

"Of course not…It was an accident. You mean no one wants anything to do with you because of an accident?" Lexi held his arm tightly and kept looking into his eyes.

"Most of these people are related. They hate me for the death of my friends. I hate myself."

"Houston, when an accident happens, whether you were doing something wrong or not, you must learn to forgive yourself," Lexi turned Houston and put her arms around him. Houston stood without moving for a moment, and then slowly moved his arms loosely around Lexi's waist. They stood that way for a few minutes, and then Lexi sat down and patted the stones for Houston to sit down also.

Lexi realized that she sounded just like Miranda. Her mother was right. She had not killed her father either. The revelation brought a peace Lexi had not known in a very long time. She felt deeply compelled to tell Houston about her situation. When she finished, there were tears in both their eyes.

"Lexi, no one has ever talked to me like this before. Even my parents are ashamed of me."

"But that's their problem. They need to forgive themselves also. When we harbor bad feeling against ourselves like this, a lot of times we take it out on others. Try talking to your parents about it. You might find that they're blaming themselves for what happened and not realizing what they're doing to you."

"Maybe…I've never had a very close relationship with them to begin with. But I guess it wouldn't hurt. My father did keep me out of reform school."

"Try it. Whether or not this is the problem, I'll be here for you when you need me, just as you cared for me during my stupidity," Lexi said squeezing his hand.

"You are as beautiful a woman on the inside as on the outside," Houston said, lifting her hand to kiss it.

"Thank you, Houston," Lexi said as she leaned toward him and kissed his cheek.

Houston smiled. "I hate to say it, but I need to get going," he said after checking his watch. "I have a 2:30 appointment I can't miss."

They stood up and headed back to the front door.

"I hope to see you very soon," Lexi said, holding onto Houston's hand and looking into his eyes when they reached the door.

"I'm all yours. Invite me over, and I'll be here," Houston said as he gently squeezed her hand.

Lexi smiled and bit her lip. She rolled her eyes around playfully then said "Great…Tomorrow…Dinner…I'd like you to meet my mother."

"Uh, are we getting serious?" Houston teased. He grinned so wide Lexi felt short of breath.

"In more ways than one," Lexi said with a smile. Then she winked and let go of Houston's hand to open the door. "See ya tomorrow."

Houston raised one eyebrow, turned, and walked out the front door. He had a spring in his step that Lexi had never seen before. She felt oddly like stopping him and asking him to stay. It made no sense. Well, he would be back for dinner tomorrow.

Lexi went to find Miranda, who she found in the kitchen, talking to Chris.

"You're the most marvelous chef," Miranda was saying.

Chris's face was beet red, but Lexi saw that he was enjoying the attention anyway.

"I must agree," Lexi stated, startling Chris, who turned away and was about to begin preparing things for the dinner hour.

"Chris, you can have the afternoon off, with pay of course. Mom and I are going out. I know we won't find the quality of food you prepare, but I want to show my mother some new sights."

Chris smiled. "Yes, miss," he said; and left to put the food in the pantry.

"Chris, when was your last vacation?" Lexi asked, knowing that he had been there seven days a week since she had arrived at Rivenwood Manor.

"I think it was about five years ago."

"Well, that won't do. I want you to take a month off and go get some relaxation time."

Chris looked worried.

"It's an earned vacation, and you'll be paid as such. In fact, I believe a bonus is in order."

"Thank you, miss."

"No. Thank you, Chris. Your dedication and your wonderful, mouth-watering food is more than I deserve."

Miranda smiled excitedly. "Can I help you plan your vacation? I won't try to talk you into anything, but I am pretty good at suggestions."

"Thank you. I wouldn't know where to start. I can really use the help," Chris smiled gratefully.

"Wonderful." Miranda grabbed a pen and pad of paper from a drawer and sat at the kitchen table. Chris laughed and went to join her so they could start planning.

Lexi felt so good. She knew it was time to look after the other servants also. She knew they had also worked round the clock for quite some time. They had days off but no real vacations. She decided they all deserved a good, relaxing vacation. Even Burdia was doing a nice job of running things smoothly. She definitely deserved some time off.

Lexi called a meeting of all the servants in the sun-room. They all came with perplexed looks on their faces, all but Chris, who knew what was up.

"Please, all of you have a seat."

This really made them confused. No other mistress had ever been this friendly, except for Miss Camilla who had gotten like that toward the end and had changed so drastically. They sat down and listened intently while their new mistress told them that they had worked so hard for so long and without complaint. She was giving them all a month off with pay, a bonus, and her mother would gladly help them plan any vacation they had in mind if they so chose.

The room was very quiet.

Then Burdia stood up and asked, "What about the house, miss? It needs taking care of."

"Of course; I will leave it in your very able hands to find a caretaker while you're gone."

"What about you, miss? Who will attend to you?" Her face reflected her satisfaction with Lexi's confidence in her.

"That won't be a problem. Mother and I will stay at the country club. There's so much to do there. We'll have a great time."

"Lexi, that sounds wonderful," Miranda said as she clasped her hands together.

"It's a beautiful place, Mom. It has swimming pools, gardens, and even its own theater. It'll be so much fun."

"It really sounds like fun, just us girls having the time of our lives at the country club," Miranda smiled happily at her daughter. Lexi smiled back and realized that this was something she would never have believed just months ago. She actually wanted to spend time with her mother.

"But, miss?" Burdia's eyes held a perplexed look.

"Burdia?"

"Why do the servants get to go? What about the mistress of the house?"

Lexi felt a strong liking for Burdia she had never felt before.

"Well, I have been pretty much on vacation since coming to Rivenwood Manor. You all have not had vacations in too long a time. It's only fair."

Burdia then did something that both shocked and made Lexi feel wonderful. She hugged Lexi and planted a kiss on her cheek before saying, "Our miss has become our mistress, and a truly godly one."

Lexi hugged Burdia back; and then everyone was excused, wiping their eyes free of the joyful tears that the scene had caused.

Later that evening, Lexi and Miranda were sitting out on the patio, sipping lemonade and watching waves crash on the shore.

"Lexi, you're changing at a very fast rate. Honey, I want you to be careful of the things you do. I mean, they're wonderful. Don't get me wrong. But I want more than anything else for you to be happy with things and never regret anything."

"Mom, I know. I just have so much inside me that needs to get out. I've done a lot of selfish things during my life, and I feel so horrible about all of it. This helps me feel better. And it's not just that. I love seeing other people happy. I never knew what kind of feeling that gives a person. It's the feeling I've looked for all my life but thought it would be found in money. In a way, I guess it has been. Not by spending it on myself, but by giving it away."

"I see your point. But at the same time, God works these things out. We need to pay attention to what he is saying. We can't know what another will do with a large sum of money, but God does. Honey, I know you don't want to go to church, and I'm not going to push you, but please pray about this money and see what kind of answer God gives you. He gave you this money for a reason."

Lexi stared at Miranda. Not once had she thought that God had given her the money. She never thought in those terms.

"All right, Mama. I will. I think that's very good advice. I'll pray tonight and tomorrow, and I'll keep praying until I know exactly what God wants me to do with all this money. I can feel there's a purpose. It's not my own selfish wants but something much bigger and something that'll make me very happy, so it must be something to do with making people happy."

Miranda smiled brightly. "My little Lexi is becoming a very mature and generous person. I saw that in you as a child. You were only three, but you made sure all the kids at your third birthday got equal-sized pieces of cake."

"Well, I guess I started out all right. Maybe I'll end up okay too, huh?"

Miranda hugged Lexi as they got up to turn in for the night.

The next day seemed to drag for Lexi. She couldn't stop thinking about Houston. She had never felt like this before. She was anxious, excited, and a bit terrified. These feelings made no sense to her at all. She had known Houston for a long time; but until yesterday, she had never actually had a conversation with him. She felt very close to him after their afternoon together, and that was a foreign feeling to her. She decided to talk to Miranda about them.

She found her mother playing with Demetri in the sunroom. Lexi had found out that Demetri loved choco-late, had a thing for dinosaurs, and loved Miranda like a grandmother. Miranda played with him for hours while he was there. They built Lego towers and bridges. They raced cars and watched the train go around and around. Miranda seemed happiest when she was with Demetri.

"Mom, can I borrow you for a moment?"

Miranda looked at Demetri.

"It's 'kay, Mirry. I keep playin.'" Demetri dismissed her gently with a kiss on the cheek.

Lexi's eyes welled up with the sweetness of the ges-ture. Demi, as they had begun to call him, really was a special little boy.

They walked to the far end of the sunroom for privacy. They sat on the long, dark blue velvet sofa that seemed to swallow every ache or pain your body could possibly have.

"Mom, I feel kind of awkward talking about this. It's not something I have any experience with and feel like I should at my age."

"What is it, honey? Whatever it is, I'm sure we can figure it out." Miranda patted Lexi's folded hands.

Lexi exhaled a deeply held breath.

"Remember I told you about Houston and that he's coming for dinner tonight?"

"Yes. In fact, I saw him leaving yesterday. He's a very handsome young man."

"Yes, he is," Lexi said with wide eyes. "He's also a very dear friend, one of the few friends I have that's my age. Anyway, I'm having a very hard time getting through this day. I can't wait for it to be dinnertime. And at the same time, I'm terrified of seeing him again. It makes no sense. I've spent many hours with him and the others. I just don't understand why I'm feeling like this."

"Honey, have you ever had a boyfriend? I don't seem to remember you ever talking about a particular boy," Miranda said with a squinting smile.

"No. Not really. I was never interested. There was a guy in school, but he had his head in the clouds, and I just didn't have time for that. We dated a few times, but there was no point in it. We had nothing in common," Lexi said with a shrug.

"Well, dear, I think you have gotten to know Houston well enough to be interested in him. I believe you like the young man more than you have ever liked anyone before. These are classic symptoms of a crush. But you being older, I think you might have found your first real boyfriend," Miranda said and smiled as she pushed a lock of Lexi's hair behind her ear.

Lexi giggled and rolled her eyes. "Oh, Mom, you've got to be kidding."

"Nope…"

"I can't believe that's how it feels. I'm going to feel so goofy tonight," Lexi said as she looked up in concerned thought.

"No, dear. Just dress comfortably but beautifully. I believe the feeling's mutual."

"Why do you say that," Lexi asked as her gaze came back abruptly to Miranda.

"He's coming to dinner to meet an old lady just to have dinner with you."

They both laughed heartily.

As 5:00 p.m. rolled around, Lexi took a hot, perfumed bath, painted her nails, styled her hair, and put on a beautiful, comfortable dress as Miranda had told her to do. She looked in the mirror and liked what she saw.

The light lavender shirt dress she chose showed off her barely faded summer tan. She wore a small rose pendent on a delicate silver chain. Her chestnut hair was pulled up into a ponytail that fell loose down her back, and she had pulled little tufts of hair out around her face and curled them. She knew she looked very feminine and felt comfortable. She now felt ready to have dinner with Houston and her mother.

It was true that Houston had not even hesitated to accept the invitation when Lexi suggested they have dinner with her mother. Maybe he liked her the way she did him. Wouldn't that be something, she thought. She had always thought men were just a trinket you adorned yourself with once you were set in life, if you were smart. She never saw herself as half of a couple like her parents. They really loved each other and had always enjoyed being together. It was obvious to everyone around them. Lexi had never been interested in that kind of relationship—at least not until now. Was she really ready for something like this? She decided she would add that to her prayer list.

She had prayed for about an hour the night before, asking God what he wanted her to do with all the money. She still had not received an answer. Then again, she was not used to praying, and she didn't know how God answered people. She would have to ask her mother. Miranda would know.

There was a knock at her door, and her mother walked in.

"Lexi, Houston's in the great room, waiting for us to come down."

Lexi felt like a thousand butterflies had just been let loose in her stomach. She felt her heart racing, and thoughts started fighting for space in her head. She looked at the door, then reached for the knob and hesitated. She stepped back to the mirror, smoothed her hair, and looked herself over from head to toe. She realized she was still barefoot, giggled, and put on her lavender house shoes.

"Dear, you look terrified," Miranda said, touching Lexi's arm lovingly.

"Well, that's one of the emotions I'm feeling," Lexi said, tossing her hands into the air slightly.

"You'll be just fine. Houston's the same person you talked to so easily yesterday. He's still the same," Miranda said, patting her arm reassuringly. Then she took Lexi's hand and led her out to the hall.

"But I'm not," Lexi whispered as they reached the staircase.

Houston was admiring a painting of one of Lexi's long-ago ancestors that hung over the huge fireplace in the great room. He turned as Lexi and Miranda entered the room. His eyes locked on Lexi, which did not help her sudden shyness.

Miranda saw this and came to the rescue.

"You must be Houston. I've heard such good things about you."

"Good to meet you, Mrs. Hunter." Houston took Miranda's hand; and a slight, friendly smile touched his lips.

"It's very good to meet you too. Shall we build a cozy fire?"

"That's sound great. It's rather chilly out tonight," Houston said with a bit more of a smile.

Miranda rang for Raymond, who quickly and effortlessly built a large fire that warmed the room quickly.

Miranda took Houston's arm and led him to a dark red, velvet-covered sofa. They sat as Lexi walked over to a chair near the sofa.

"You look very beautiful tonight, Lexi," Houston said as he gazed at her.

"So do you. I mean, you look very nice tonight too, Houston." Lexi could feel her face turning crimson.

Houston had on a cream colored long sleeved shirt that went perfectly with his honey colored skin. His black hair was slicked back with a few stands loose over his forehead. His black jeans looked brand new. He looked ready for a formal or informal meeting at the same time.

"Thank you," Houston said with the largest grin Lexi had ever seen on his face.

Oddly enough, the grin actually helped Lexi overcome her embarrassment.

"Have you seen any of the group? I'm really worried about Appel. She always seems so together, but it's just a wall she has built up, you know? And I haven't been able to get hold of her," Lexi said, going with the strength of conversation unrelated to their looks.

"Appel's in rehab. From what I heard, when she found out that you were stopping the party scene, she decided she should also. I think you are the only one she actually liked of the group," Houston said as he sat forward, his hands clasped in front of him.

"Oh, I am so happy to hear that," Lexi said with a large smile of her own.

"If you'd like, we could go visit her once she's allowed visits. They have a step program there, and she has to earn everything."

"Yes. I would love to."

"Isn't it amazing the way the Lord works?" Miranda sighed.

Lexi felt a zing go through her heart, not knowing how Houston would react to her mother's mention of God.

"Yes. It's truly amazing sometimes. My grandmother used to say that all bad turns to good for those who love the Lord. I've seen it myself."

"I'm so happy you are a godly man, Houston. I find it very distressing the way our society has turned its back on God."

Houston looked at Miranda and nodded his head in understanding.

"It's very sad. They doom themselves, and for what? For money that lasts the years of your life and no further.

It's sad and frightening," Houston said, shaking his head in disdain.

Lexi sat back and listened and learned a few things as Miranda and Houston discussed God. She was truly amazed that Houston had such deep faith. Even after their conversation yesterday, Lexi had no clue that he was a Christian. Maybe he did not want to scare her away if she had no faith.

After half an hour of visiting, Raymond came to announce that dinner was ready. The three got up and made their way to the dining room.

"I love this house. It's so elegant, but yet it's not gaudy like a lot of the other estates I've been to. It's really classy," Houston said as he looked around, nodding approvingly.

"I can take no credit. My ancestors and Aunt Camilla were the one who decorated this house. They knew class when they saw it." Lexi smiled at the memory of her aunt. It made her feel comforted to know that Camilla had become a Christian. Then, suddenly, Lexi realized that since her father's death, she had been leaning more and more that way; and after listening to Miranda and Houston, she decided she wanted to know even more.

Once they were seated and served, Miranda said grace. The three echoed, "Amen," together; and then Lexi looked at Houston.

"Houston, would you like to attend church with my mother and me this Sunday?"

Miranda dropped her fork, causing Houston and Lexi to look at her.

"Oh, I'm so excited. Lexi, you don't know how long I've waited to hear you say that you wanted to go to church."

"Well, listening to you and Houston just now made me realize that I don't know much and that I definitely want to know more," Lexi said. She paused and looked thoughtfully upward. She looked pointedly back at Houston and Miranda. "I mean, I remember all the basic stuff from Sunday school, like David and Goliath and things like that, but I want to know how to pray and how to know when God is telling you something or how he answers people. I didn't learn that in Sunday school that I can remember."

"Lexi, God answers our prayers in different ways. But one thing is for sure. If we're paying attention, we know when he's answering." Her mother smiled at her.

"So, Houston, would you like to go with us?"

"Yes. I'd love to. I haven't been to church since I don't know when, but I've been feeling that I'd like to start going again just lately. I can't explain why, but there's this nagging at me."

"The Holy Spirit," Miranda said with a nod.

"You're probably right about that." Houston smiled.

They chatted about growing up going to church and how Lexi's small-town church differed from the huge, richly decorated church Houston attended growing up. But one thing remained the same: they were both Bible-based churches and had biblical teachings.

When the meal was done, they went back into the great room to relax by the fire. Houston sat next to Lexi on the couch this time, and Miranda sat in the chair. They talked for a couple of hours about anything and everything, and then Miranda excused herself to go up to bed.

"I hadn't realized it's so late," Houston apologized as he looked at his watch.

"No. It's all right. I haven't enjoyed an evening like this in…well, I don't think I ever have," Lexi said quickly. "I never realized what I was missing, always thinking about money and how to make it and then recently how to spend it on myself. That really is such a waste of time."

"It's a very mature way of thinking. I guess I came to that realization after the accident. Life is too short and can be taken away at any time. It's how we live, how we help, and the person we are inside that really counts." Lexi smiled at him and moved closer to him on the couch. Houston put his arm around her and pulled her close to him.

"Yes, exactly…I never thought like this 'till my father passed away. I never thought anyone I knew would ever really die, you know? This life is temporary, but we honestly don't believe that. And when we lose a loved one, I guess it shocks us back into reality for a while." Lexi looked up into Houston's eyes before she continued. "I want to remember what it's taught me. I want to put others before myself. How horrible it feels not to do that and then lose a person…"

Houston tightened his arm around her for a moment then pushed a curl behind her ear affectionately.

"It's good to come to this realization at our age. Some people never come to it, and they die so agonizingly. It's truly sad when that happens."

"Yeah, I'm so happy my father knew the truth."

They both stared at the fire, each with their own thoughts.

"Lexi, I want to tell you something, but I don't want to make you feel uncomfortable around me," Houston said hesitantly.

"To be honest, I was very uncomfortable earlier, but that's gone away. Please tell me," Lexi said, sitting up and facing him. She folded her hands in her lap and waited.

"I really care for you, more than I've ever cared for a woman. I felt like a kid with my first crush on my way over here, all nervous and awkward…" Houston face darkened and his stared at the floor.

Lexi laughed until she had tears in her eyes. She laughed so hard she fell to her side away from Houston.

"I don't see what's so funny." Houston sat up straight. He was clearly upset at her reaction.

"No…I have to…tell you…Me too," Lexi gasped out between laughs. She felt hysterical. The relief was so great that she couldn't stop laughing.

Houston stared at her, embarrassment and hurt plain on his face until the sudden realization of what she said hit him; and his face cleared, and a large grin appeared before he ended up laughing with her.

"Wow. Can you believe it? You own all of this. I'm an heir to a fortune, and we were afraid…to let each other know…we're smitten," Houston said between gasps for air as he kept wiping tears of laughter from his eyes.

They laughed until it died away, and then Houston took Lexi in his arms and kissed her gently. It was the most wonderful thing Lexi had ever felt. She wrapped her arms around him, and they kissed for what seemed forever and yet it ended far too soon.

They talked for another hour, about things near to their hearts, as they got to know each other better.

Lexi glanced at the clock and saw that it was almost 3:00 a.m. She couldn't believe how the time had flown. When Houston saw Lexi's expression, he looked at the clock.

"I should be going. I have to help my mother with a few things in the morning. She'll want me awake to do that," Houston said and winked with a smile.

"Okay. I'm looking forward to church this Sunday. But you can always drop by anytime," Lexi said as she stood up. She put her arms around Houston when they stood up and put her head against his chest.

"I'll be here so often you'll get sick of me," he said as he wrapped his arms around her and kissed the top of her head.

"Not likely," Lexi said as forcefully as she could while yawning.

They walked out to the front door, smiling and holding hands. Houston kissed Lexi good night and left. Lexi seemed to float up to her bedroom.

The next morning, Miranda helped different staff members tie up the loose ends on their vacation plans; and Lexi called the country club to make sure everything was ready for her mother's and her time there. She knew it would be. They cleaned the apartments every day whether people were there or not, and they kept fresh food for anyone who mentioned being there. Not that they needed to since the chef and beautiful dining room at the club would make it foolish for anyone to cook their own food. Lexi wanted to make sure Miranda had a wonderful time.

Lexi looked at herself in the mirror. How much she had changed. She realized that her father's death had made her grow up in so many ways—but not just that. She had become a new person. She took a few minutes to thank her dad mentally for the things he taught her when she was young. They were all the right things. Even though she had turned away from them and from her mother's teachings of God, she was now returning to a place that felt comfortable and right. She felt the joy of her childhood returning. She never realized the joy she had when she was little; nor did she realize when it disappeared. Having it back, even to a slight degree, was something she wanted to maintain for the rest of her life. She knew it was because she was opening up to God. She knew he had never left her. It had been she who had run away from him. That was changing at an incredible speed, and it felt good.

She got on her knees by the side of her bed and said a prayer of thanks to God for all he was showing her. She thanked him for all the blessings she was receiving and for taking care of her dad in heaven. She now knew that her dad was not lost to her forever but that she would see him again one day. It would be in a wondrous place, where no pain or suffering could ever interfere or take away their joy. She knew it in her heart as well as her head.

Lexi took a quick shower. Then she joined Miranda for the last of Chris's cooking for a month. It was a happy affair, with croissants and pastries—the likes Lexi had never seen or tasted before.

"Careful, Chris. We might not let you leave," Lexi joked after consuming one too many of the croissants. She washed it down with a large mug of smooth coffee and patted her full stomach. "I could become very overweight with you around."

"Oh, but I watch the menu for you." Chris smiled happily.

"Yes. You are a gem."

Chris blushed happily. He said his good-byes and then made his exit to his quarters to finish packing and get ready for his taxi to the airport.

Lexi and Miranda walked into the great room to start a fire. It was quite chilly for a late September morning, but the coziness of a fire sounded so good that they were happy about the chill. Lexi had learned from Raymond how to build and stoke the fire. She decided that she didn't need to be waited on hand and foot for every little thing. She just needed the servants to take care of the huge house when she couldn't. She knew she was definitely changing into a better person; and it made her feel good.

Lexi smiled and hummed as she worked on stoking the fire. When she had brought the fire to a comfortable blaze, she walked to the sofa, kissed Miranda's cheek, and sat down.

"Honey, you look so full of peace. It's amazing. I remember the day you came to the house after Daddy died. You were so tormented. It showed so much on your face. It makes me feel so much better the peace I see there now," Miranda said as she patted Lexi's folded hands.

"Yeah, I was a real mess. I had probably run as far from God as I could get. I was doing so many things I shouldn't, just trying to occupy my useless life," Lexi said as she stared into the fire, her eyes thoughtful as she remembered the past.

"I was just spending money on myself and pampering myself. That got old so quick." Lexi looked into Miranda's eyes. "And to think that's all I dreamed of for years. But it's a dream that's not based in reality. Now I don't exactly know what I'm meant to do, but I know it won't involve spoiling myself."

Lexi smiled as she took Miranda's hands in hers and gently rubbed them in affection.

"You still don't know what it is that God has brought you to this place in your life for, huh?"

"No. He could be telling me, but I don't know how to listen yet maybe. I know I need to learn a lot more about God. I need to be a lot closer to him." Lexi looked back at the fire, her brows furled with thought.

"It's Jesus you need to be a lot closer to. You need to develop your personal relationship with Jesus," Miranda said, taking Lexi's chin and gently turning her head to meet her eyes.

"Jesus is God, right? It's been so long. I'm kind of confused." Lexi tilted her head slightly.

"Jesus is God, yes. God is the Father, the Son, and the Holy Spirit. Many people are confused on this subject. I find it easiest to say God is like government. Government is one thing, but there are many people in government, just as God is one, and yet three. However, government is very imperfect, where God is perfection. And the will of God is perfect. They are always in perfect agreement, of one mind, perfect synchronization, if you will. Does that help?"

"Yes. That makes sense," Lexi said. Her face cleared a bit with understanding.

"It's more complicated. But for us humans, it's the easiest way to think about the trinity. My minister told me that when I was young, and I have always remembered it."

"I'm so happy I have you to help me, Mama."

Lexi could see in Miranda's eyes the surge of love that she was feeling. Lexi hadn't called her Mama since she was very young. She had always called her Mother since growing up. It was a label that had a disrespectful tone every time she had said it. Now it was always Mama, like when she was young. Lexi knew if she ever called her Mother again, it would be in a much more respectful and loving tone than before.

"So am I, sweetie. So am I."

The phone rang, and broke into their quiet time. It was Houston.

"Hi, Lexi. I found out Appel can have visitors starting today. Do you want to go with me to see her?"

"Oh yes! That would be great. What time are you planning to go?"

"I can be there in about half an hour if that's good for you."

"Sure thing. I can't wait to see Appel."

"I know. I feel the same way."

"K. I'll see you then."

"Bye, Lexi."

After Lexi got ready for her visit, she explained to Miranda about Appel. She told her they would be going to see her and that she wanted to talk to her about God.

"Honey, that's wonderful. Only…"

"Only what?"

"Be careful. If you come on too strong, you could push her away. Just maybe mention that you are learning about God. Leave it at that. Let her get interested by watching the transformation in you. Let her ask questions. I have learned what trying too hard can do."

Lexi realized that her mother was talking about her. She also realized her mother had a lot of wisdom.

"All right, Mama. I see what you mean. And you're right. I don't want to turn her off. I'll take it slow. Thanks, Mama." Lexi kissed her cheek and went to get the door as the doorbell chimed Houston's arrival.

Houston greeted Miranda. Then he and Lexi said their good-byes and left to visit Appel.

The drive to Shady River, the facility that Appel had checked herself into, was two hours long. However, to Lexi, it seemed rather short, as she and Houston talked and laughed and got to know each other even more.

She was surprised at how easily she and Houston were able to talk and how comfortable she felt with him now that they had gotten their feelings out into the open. Chalk another one up for honesty, Lexi thought.

"Well, here we are. I'm so happy Appel has done this. I just hope she's feeling as happy," Houston said with a little concern in his voice.

"I know what you mean. I've been wondering myself if she's regretting this. I hope not."

They walked in holding hands. They came to an information desk just inside the door. An older, heavy-set woman with large teeth and graying hair greeted them.

"Can I help you?"

"Yes. We would like to visit with Appel Broughter. I called earlier and was told she could have visits today from 3:00 p.m. to 6:00 p.m.," Houston said with a professional air.

The woman typed a few things into her computer and then said, "Ah. Yes. Miss Broughter will be in room 15C. Take that elevator to the third floor. And as you exit, take a right. Go down to the seventh door on the left, that's 15C. It also has a plaque above the door, so you can't miss it," the woman smiled brightly at Houston.

"Thank you," Houston said with a slight bow of his head.

Lexi and Houston found 15C with no trouble. They entered a large room with a few groups of people talking and laughing. They saw a couch with three chairs in one corner and walked over to claim that area.

It seemed to take forever before Appel came into the room and looked around. As soon as she saw Lexi and Houston, her face broke into the biggest smile Lexi had ever seen on Appel's face.

She hurried over and hugged both of them tightly.

"Guys, thank you so much for visiting me. I feel so alone here. I hate this place, but I guess it's a necessary evil. I probably should have quit on my own."

"I think you did the right thing, Appel. I'm so happy you're doing all right. You are, right?" Lexi reached out and took Appel's hand and looked into her eyes intently.

"Yes, little Lexi." Appel squeezed Lexi's hand and smile. She had given Lexi that nickname since she had been the shortest person in the group. She also saw her as a little sister.

Appel shook her head, and her blond curls shook. Her eyes were crystal blue today and had a sparkle.

They all sat down and got comfortable. Lexi and Houston sat at the end of the couch closest to the chair Appel sat in.

"So how's everyone? Or are ya in touch with any of the old group?" Appel looked at them apprehensively, concern wrinkling her forehead. Her family had been vacationing in Europe since just after Lexi's father had died. Although she knew Lexi had stopped partying, she wouldn't know much else, including if Lexi had started again or not.

"No. We haven't been in touch with anyone from the group. They have called me several times, inquiring about Lexi and I joining them for a party here and there. But I just let them know we're not interested anymore. It's too hard to watch what they do," Houston said, shaking his head and looking down at the floor.

"Yeah, I can see why now. I hope they all come to their senses and straighten up before they end up being buried by their partying. I don't think anyone knows the main reason I came here," Appel paused and put her fist to her mouth. She stared out the window a moment before she continued.

"My cousin Lissa was killed in an accident. She and her friends were out partying on her friend's yacht. They ran into another boat that exploded and there were no survivors."

Lexi saw that Appel's eyes were getting very teary. Lexi squeezed her hand, and Appel shook her head and her eyes cleared up.

"Anyway, my parents, for the first time in my life, put their foot down. I kinda liked it. Now I know they want me around."

"That helps. I know if you don't feel wanted, it's very hard to care for yourself," Houston said knowingly with a tone. Lexi rubbed one finger lovingly over his hand in support.

"Yep, now I know they care, so I care. Plus I know you both care for me, and I care for you. I must ask something though. I keep seeing you two look at each other kind of strangely. Is there something going on? Come on. You have to tell me."

Lexi and Houston looked at each other and grinned.

"Lexi and I have started seeing each other," Houston said as he took Lexi's hand.

"I knew it! Oh, guys, this is awesome. I always thought you two would be perfect for each other." Appel got up and hugged them both.

"Oh yeah," Lexi asked. "If that's true, why didn't you tell me?" She laughed happily.

"Well, I knew you wouldn't listen," Appel rolled her eyes. "You never listened to me. Every time I gave you advice, you did the opposite."

"Yeah, that's pretty much true." Lexi smiled at the memory.

"This is just too great. You two have made my day."

Lexi and Houston looked at each other and knew the other was also wondering why Appel was happy about them as a couple.

Appel saw the look and explained.

"I know a bit about each of you, and I have always liked you two best out of the group. You're both good people and deserve to be with good people. I also love it when I get my way." Appel laughed heartily.

Lexi and Houston laughed.

"Well, I'm so happy we were able to give you the good news in person then. I love to see you smile, Appel," Lexi said with a loving smile.

"Oh, me too…I wasn't expecting anyone to visit today since my parents are off in Europe somewhere. But I was hoping. Another wish came true when you two showed up."

They talked for a couple hours, and then Lexi felt comfortable opening a different kind of door in the conversation.

"Appel, you won't believe this. But Houston and I are going to church with my mother on Sunday."

Appel's jaw dropped. She was very quiet for about two minutes and then started the questions.

"Your mother...I thought you and she were kind of on the outs? Church, when did you start getting religious? Houston? Church?"

Her questions went on and on for about fifteen minutes, Lexi and Houston answering in short, to-the-point answers—enough, they knew, to satisfy her curiosity but not too much as to turn her off.

"Huh. Maybe one of these days you can tell me a little more. Now how about telling me some more about the two of you? You just started dating?"

"Yes," answered Houston; and they talked about future events they would like to do together and with Appel.

When it came time to leave, all three were relaxed and happy from a very good visit. Appel had decided Lexi was right and that she had made the right decision to come to the clinic. She told Lexi and Houston she was going to really start participating with the doctors and staff so she could get well and come home. They hugged good-bye with the promise of another visit soon.

Miranda was waiting for them in the great room when they got back to Rivenwood. She rushed out to greet them as they walked through the door, taking their coats and handing them to Raymond with a smile.

"Please come into the great room. I have a large fire going."

Lexi and Houston followed Miranda and saw a beautiful blaze much bigger than Lexi had built that morning. The fireplace was huge and could contain a small or quite large fire. Miranda had built almost to the fireplace's capacity.

"This is very cozy, Mom, but why such a big fire?"

"It was pretty chilly, and I knew you two would be tired out from your drive. Have a seat. I made some warm apple cider with cinnamon sticks."

Lexi remembered her mother's love of fall and how she loved to bake for and feed her family.

"Does this mean there is maybe a homemade apple pie somewhere in the house?" Lexi teased, but at the same time hoped the answer was yes.

"Well, of course."

"Houston, Mom makes the best pies. And wait 'till you taste this cider."

Houston took a sip gingerly then took a full swallow.

"Wow. This is amazing. I've never cared for apple cider, but this is delicious."

Miranda beamed with the praise.

"Okay, why all the special treatment?" Lexi asked.

"I went for a walk around the grounds today, and the fall spirit just hit me. I got a chill and then wanted to surprise you with the big fire. I was also thinking we should find a place to get a pumpkin and take Demi. He's never had a real Halloween. I know he would just love it."

Lexi felt a thrill surge through her at the idea.

"That's a wonderful idea, Mom. Since Abbey and Demi will be staying at the country club also, it'll give Abbey some time to rest and Demi a chance to run around and wear off some of his energy."

"I'm so happy you agree."

"How about after we get settled at the country club Monday morning, we start hunting the Internet for some pumpkin patches?"

"I know of a great one," Houston said, catching the excitement. "My parents took me there as a kid, and I go every year just to look around."

"Then I guess we don't have to search," Lexi said with a happy giggle. "This is going to be so much fun."

The rest of the evening they spent enjoying Miranda's cooking and packing things for their stay at the country club. Houston helped by bringing boxes down to Raymond so he didn't have to tire himself out going up and down stairs and out to the limousine.

When they were done packing, they had more apple pie with melted caramel drizzled over the top. It was a good, satisfying treat.

Houston left to let Miranda and Lexi have some time alone before church the next morning. They used the time to take a swim in Miranda's large tub before bed.

"Mom, I don't know why, but I'm feeling a little anxious about church tomorrow," Lexi said as she pulled herself out of the water and sat on the bath couch. Miranda pulled herself up to sit next to Lexi.

"Maybe it's because it's been a while since you've been there."

"Maybe…How's the minister? Is he interesting? I remember Pastor Herrol. He was so boring that when I tried to pay attention, I'd have a hard time not falling asleep," Lexi said dejectedly.

"Well, you were little then and didn't understand what he was talking about. He was actually quite good. I guess you'll need to hear this minister to form an opinion. But I really like him. He has a good sense of humor. That keeps sermons fun and interesting," Miranda said and patted Lexi's knee. Lexi smiled.

Lexi thought that it was a good thing for a minister to have a sense of humor. This world was so sad. If a minister could make it a little better place by a smile here and there, so much the better.

Chapter 9

*L*exi woke early the next morning. She had an excitement flowing through her she didn't quite know how to feel about. It did feel good, so she didn't think about it too much, just enjoyed it.

She came downstairs to find Miranda in the kitchen, cooking omelets and making toast. She had fresh-squeezed orange juice in a pitcher and a plate of fresh-baked cinnamon rolls on the counter.

"Wow, Mom. How are we going to eat all of this?"

"Well, I intend to help." Houston walked in from the dining room with a large grin on his face.

Lexi thought about the fact that she had never seen Houston smile much. In fact, it was always a smirk up until recently; and now he seemed to smile all the time. It made her heart break, and at the same time it felt as if it did a flip in her chest. She felt a sudden, very strong love inside for this man. She was falling in love with Houston. Her mother was right. She didn't have to ask advice about this feeling. She knew what it was.

"Well, hello there. If I had known you would be here so early I would have dressed."

Lexi had on an old tee shirt; sweat pants; oversized socks; and a dark green, terrycloth robe. Her hair was piled on her head with bobby pins, and many strands stuck out wildly. She knew she was a mess. Not a speck of makeup either. Since Miranda had come to live with her, she had given up the fancy, not-very-comfortable loungewear for night clothing similar to her childhood slob clothes.

"Well, if I had known how good you can make old clothes look, I would have told you to wear them sooner," Houston said with a teasing but caring grin.

"Yeah…right. I'll be back down shortly."

Lexi ran up to shower and change after she gave Houston a quick kiss. She did all that and put on her makeup in record time and was back down to the dining room as Miranda and Houston finished putting the food on the table.

"Wow. That was quick," Houston said happily.

"Well, I guess the smell of the food and the good company down here just worked magic with me." Lexi smiled.

They ate and talked about the church they were going to. Houston said he had seen the church but had never gone to it. He went to his family's church near his home when he was young but had stopped going not because of God but because the people there were not very nice to him after the accident.

"It's sad that some people don't listen to God when he tells us straight-out not to judge others. Only he is able to do that because we can't possibly know everything involved. But he does. He knows our hearts," Miranda said.

They arrived at the church at 10:30 a.m. The service started in fifteen minutes. Miranda led the way to the second pew from the front.

"You always sit up front, Mama?" Lexi asked a bit self-consciously.

"Yes. I want to make sure I can hear everything."

They sat down, and Lexi noticed that her mother was marking all the pages in the hymnal that were noted up on a board. She remembered the number plaque from her childhood church.

Lexi followed her mother's lead and started marking pages.

"Good morning, Miranda," a voice boomed to Lexi's right. A large man with a happy face reached out and shook Miranda's hand.

"Good morning, Reverend. It sure is a beautiful day, isn't it?"

"Yes. I love the cooler weather. Makes people not as anxious to get out of the hot church." He laughed heartily.

"Reverend Wallace, I'd like to introduce you to my daughter, Lexi, and her friend, Houston Cheyenne."

The minister shook their hands but paused when he shook Houston's.

"You seem familiar. Ah. I remember now. I am so sorry of the tragedy that befell you and your friends so long ago. I'm very happy to see it did not create a riff between you and the Lord. That does happen sometimes."

Houston was stunned. Not only that someone he never met remembered the accident, but he didn't see him as a monster.

"I should explain," Reverend Wallace continued at Houston's look of confusion. "I counseled your mother after the accident. I was working at St Peter's church back then as resident counselor."

Houston's face relaxed a little, and he smiled. "It's nice to meet you, Reverend."

The organist played an old-time hymn.

"Well, that's my cue to get ready. I'm so happy to have you three here."

With that, he turned around and disappeared through a dark red, velvet drape-covered doorway.

The service started with an old hymn that was vaguely familiar to Lexi. She felt a kind of strange homesickness. That was the only feeling she could compare the feeling to.

The sermon was very good. Pastor Wallace talked about how mistakes we make are most of the time sins and that we can be forgiven. She noticed that Houston was listening intently to the sermon, his eyes never leaving the minister. She diverted her attention to the minister and found concentration on the sermon was not difficult.

The sermon seemed to end too soon, and it shocked Lexi that she would feel that way. It was very odd. She remembered as a child feeling that a sermon seemed to go on for hours.

At the end of the service, the pastor walked to the back of the church to shake everyone's hand as they left. He asked Lexi and Houston to please come back, and they said they definitely would. And they actually meant it.

Lexi was quiet all the way home, so much so that finally Houston broke the silence.

"That was a very good sermon, don't you think, Lexi?"

"Yes. I kind of keep replaying certain parts in my head. I like that I came away from there knowing a little more. Is it always like that, Mom?"

"No. Sometimes it reaffirms what you already know, sometimes it calls into question things you think you know, sometimes it leaves you with a bad feeling when the Holy Spirit is convicting you of a sin you have not repented of, and sometimes it just leaves you with a good feeling. It all depends on where you are with God."

"No matter where you are in your faith, you really need church, huh?"

"I believe that."

They talked about God and church the rest of the way to the country club.

When she saw the country club, Miranda was thrilled.

"This is going to be so much fun. Lexi told me all about this place. We can even go shopping and not leave the grounds," Miranda exclaimed as she took Houston's arm. She chattered like a bird all the way to their apartment.

When Lexi unlocked the door, Miranda gasped.

"This is an apartment? It's huge. And we get to use it just because why?"

"Aunt Cami contributed a large amount of the money that built this place and now maintains it. So you could say it kind of goes with the house." Lexi smiled.

"She really lived it up, didn't she," Miranda said with a sigh.

Reeves and Houston brought everything inside from the car as Lexi and Miranda unpacked.

Once they had finished unloading the car, Reeves left for his vacation with a few happy words and hugs. Lexi and Miranda would use the country club's car and chauffer during their stay.

When Lexi and Miranda had finished unpacking, Lexi turned to Miranda.

"Mom, I've wondered, why me? Why didn't she leave the money to Daddy?"

"He told her he didn't want it," Miranda said with a shrug.

"What? She was going to give it to Daddy? Why didn't he want it," Lexi asked a few tones higher than she normally spoke. Her eyes were wide and mouth agape.

"Money can change people for the worst. Your father was happy with our life," Miranda said with a peaceful smile.

"And you were happy too," Lexi ask, her head tilting slightly to one side trying to understand.

"Well, at first, I fought him on it." Lexi's head dropped slightly, and she leaned in to stare at Miranda. "Yes Lexi." Her mother smiled at her surprise. "I fought him hard. I wanted the money. We almost split up over it. But God showed me something I have never forgotten. He showed me what a wonderful man your father was. He showed me that your father knew what he was doing."

"So why did Aunt Cami leave it to me then?" Lexi shook her head as if trying to unscramble her thoughts.

"Obviously, the Lord saw fit for you to have it. You know he has a plan. You just need to find out what it is," Miranda said with conviction.

"Yes. I sure do know there's something. I just can't figure out what," Lexi said, hitting her forehead lightly with the heel of her hand.

"Well, you'll find out in his time and not your own," Miranda said knowingly as she took Lexi's hand and smoothed her hair. "Don't blame yourself for not know-ing right now. You are seeking him and when the time is right, he won't let you be confused about his answer."

Lexi thought about it and knew Miranda was right. She would know what God wanted her to do when he wanted her to know. She had faith in him to take care of everything since she knew she would never be able to do it herself. She settled into a comfortable chair and watched as Houston started a fire.

Autumn was getting bitingly cold and damp. Lexi never really had a favorite time of year, but she was starting to enjoy the fall. With Miranda acting like a kid again and the almost constant presence of Houston, she was having more fun than she had ever had in her life. Even more than that, she felt content. The only thing that would make everything perfect would be if God chose to let her know what he wanted her to do with the money. She wanted to get started so badly but had no idea what to do. She only knew that it would help others.

Around 7:30 p.m. there was a knock at the door. Houston opened the door to Jeff Gary.

"Hey, guy. What the heck? We haven't seen you around in a long time, and here you are, sequestered with Lexi. What're the two of you up to?" he asked as he brushed past Houston and sauntered into the living room. He looked at Lexi with one raised eyebrow.

"Jeff, how nice to see you," Lexi stammered at the unexpected visit. Houston looked very uncomfortable, and Lexi knew there was going to be a problem.

"Well, it's nice to see you too," Jeff said with the same eyebrow raised. The sarcasm in his voice was thick. "We've all been missing you and Houston and Appel. It's not the same anymore, and we want you two to come down to the pool and party with us," Jeff said demandingly as he furrowed his eyebrows.

Lexi and Houston could tell he had already been partying for most likely the whole afternoon. Jeff was normally very diplomatic when trying to get his way when sober, but he seemed ready to use force if needed.

"Jeff, we miss you all too, but we've come to realize that we don't want to party like that anymore. It was getting out of hand," Lexi tried to explain without angering Jeff.

"Oh, so you're better than us now? You think we're out of control," Jeff asked angrily as his face turned red, and he took a step towards her.

"No, I was. Not you. I couldn't handle it," Lexi said quickly. She made her voice sound as self-loathing as possible, hoping Jeff would be convinced.

Jeff looked at her with a sneer and then shook his head.

"Fine," he said, looking her up and down as if she were something disgusting. "Be a snob. You're not worth the effort. But, Houston, bud, you can't walk out on us," he said as he swung around and put his arm around Houston. Houston slowly stepped away from Jeff while holding the door open. Lexi saw he was holding his anger in check, but his eyes were smoldering.

"Jeff, I think you'd better go," Houston said evenly with little emotion.

"No. You're one of us and always will be. Don't let that wench change you," Jeff said pleadingly, nodding his head at Lexi.

"Jeff, now," Houston said more firmly.

"Fine, but this isn't the end of this," Jeff said determinedly as he stomped out the door.

Once the shock of seeing Jeff so angry wore off and being near him without having been inebriated herself, Lexi said, "Maybe we shouldn't have come here."

"Nonsense…Your aunt just about built this place herself. If anyone shouldn't be here, it's them," Houston said through clenched teeth.

"They need some guidance. They need to know the Lord in order to change their hearts," Miranda said softly.

"Yes, but they don't want to hear about him. I tried at different times when I thought they would listen. But they don't want to know about him. It makes them feel ashamed of what they like to do, so they push him away," Houston said as he sat down on the floor by the fireplace, next to Lexi.

"Yes, that's true of a lot of people. It's so sad. In the end, they hurt themselves and all who care about them. I mean, they think they're having fun, but it's really hollow fun. No reality to it. And the fun is never worth the horrible consequences. It's so very sad," Miranda said as she slowly shook her head.

"I hope they don't intend to start trouble." Lexi got up and paced the length of the living room. She wrung her hands and looked from Houston to Miranda. Her face cleared and she said, "Maybe we should do something for them to stop it before it starts, be there for them when they wake up out of sorts and then let them know that even though we won't party anymore, it doesn't mean that we don't care."

"Excellent idea Lexi…You sure are a good person," Houston said squeezing her hand.

Lexi felt her heart swell. Houston thought she was a good person. She knew she had a lot more changing to do, but it felt good to know he thought so highly of her.

The rest of the evening the three sat talking and staying warm by the fire. They drank apple cider Miranda had made, which was a deliciously perfect mixture of tart and sweet. The cinnamon stick in each cup added to the coziness of the evening.

Lexi didn't think life could get any better than this, and it cost very little money. The cider ingredients and the logs for the fire were all that this lovely evening had really cost. They could have been in a rustic cabin for all it mattered. Most of all it was the people around her that gave her the heartwarming happiness she now felt. And all these years she had thought the only way to find true happiness was with money.

How wrong I was, Lexi thought.

She knew that if she was starving, then money would help her. To have a lot more money than she needed, it was not what made happiness. It brought no happiness sitting in a bank account, collecting interest. It would be better spent making others happy, but what others? She said a quick prayer to remind God that she was waiting on him. Then she rejoined the conversation, which had turned to driving up into the mountains to play in the snow.

"We're all going into our second childhoods, it seems." Lexi smiled and teased two of the people she loved most in the world.

They all laughed, and the room became quite as they stared into the fire.

"So what should we do to make them understand that we care, but we don't want to participate anymore?" Lexi asked quietly.

"You know, they'll all be feeling a bit under the weather tomorrow." Miranda smiled. "Why not bring them a cup of coffee, some aspirin, and a shoulder to cry on about their aches and pains just as you suggested?"

"You know, I would have loved for someone to take care of me like that some mornings," Lexi confided.

"It might not work, but we can keep trying. After all, these are the people who accepted me as I am. They didn't shut me out when everyone else did. I want to at least try," Houston said with a small smile. His attitude had change significantly from his earlier confrontation with Jeff.

The next morning, Houston came over early; and the three got going on their nurse maid plan. Everyone was exceptionally welcoming to the pampering except for Jeff, who threw them out and slammed his door.

When they returned to the apartment, Lexi said, "Well, at least the others were responsive. We'll have to work on Jeff."

"I think Jeff will be very hard-won," Houston replied.

"Why," Lexi asked, tilting her head and looking into Houston's eyes.

"Because he likes you, and you're with me. It's not that he doesn't want us together so much as he wants you worshipping at his feet. When he likes a girl, he wants her to want him more than anything in the world. I know he loves Dotty, it's really just an ego thing," Houston said with a smirk. Lexi saw that Houston disliked that part of Jeff's personality.

"Is that it? Well, maybe I need to work on that. Or maybe we need to work on it. Start telling him how hard-headed I am and that I boss you around all the time but that you can't give up because you're mad about me." Lexi smiled. "I remember how he hated the way Dotty tried to boss him around. If he thinks I'm worse than Dotty…"

"Great idea, we can even stage a confrontation to make him realize he doesn't want to be with you." Houston smiled.

"Yes. I'll be a real ogre," Lexi said baring her teeth, scrunching her face and crossing her eyes with her hands up in front of her, looking like claws.

Houston and Miranda laughed, and Lexi soon joined them.

The three plotted more as they walked back to the apartment. Lexi could not believe how much fun she was having. At the same time, she felt guilty knowing that there was something she should be doing. She had never felt so happy, nor had she ever felt so guilty for feeling happy. She just did not know what God wanted her to do.

Once they were in the apartment, Lexi excused herself to take a hot bath and talk to God. She prayed earnestly for half an hour and then felt that she should get back out with the others. She felt a new peace about the situation of knowing what God wanted. She knew he would tell her when the time was right. She just needed to leave it in his hands and have patience and faith.

Later that day, Houston and Lexi found Jeff in the solarium, reading. They pretended not to notice him there.

Lexi turned to Houston quickly and shouted, "I told you, I don't want to go to the mountains this weekend."

Houston took the hint and took up his part, talking quietly but just loud enough that Jeff would hear. "But you said you wanted to go last week."

"That was last week. I don't like to plan things so far in advance. I'd rather just go when I want," Lexi said as she folder her arms across her chest and tilted her head back a bit while looking away from Houston.

"But that's hard to plan," Houston said with a sigh as if trying to explain to a child.

"I told you I don't like to plan things. Get it in your head, Houston," Lexi said pointing her finger in his face. "We do things my way or no way. If you don't like how things are, find someone else. I have agreed to be with you because you don't annoy me as much as other people, but if you start wanting to plan things and run my life, well, then it's over!"

"I just want to make sure we can do the things you want to do. Sometimes we have to make reservations," Houston said with defeat as he lowered his head.

"Not with my money we don't," Lexi said haughtily. She put her nose high in the air and scowled extra hard to stop from smiling at the ridiculousness and knew this was exactly how the old Lexi probably would have behaved.

"Okay, so what do you want to do," Houston ask as he looked at Jeff with the blush of embarrassment on his face.

"I want to go shopping," Lexi said as she moved to stand against Houston as she'd seen Dotty do to Jeff on numerous occasions.

"We just went shopping yesterday," Houston said in a slightly irritated tone.

"Well, I want to go again. You don't mind, right?" She practically purred as she ran her hand over Houston's chest the way she had seen Dotty do to Jeff. She knew he particularly hated that.

"Okay, we will think of something else to do for the rest of the weekend," Houston said with a sigh of defeat.

"I will think of something. Just put away those old skis. I'm not too fond of skiing anyway." Lexi threw in the part about skiing knowing that Jeff lived on the slopes in the winter.

Lexi walked out, and Houston sat down with his head in his hands as if soothing a bad headache. Lexi hid behind a large plant to watch.

It wasn't long before Jeff was sitting down next to him.

"Hey Houston, sorry to see that...I thought Lexi was different," Jeff said clapping Houston on the back.

"Hi Jeff...She is different. I mean...well, she just has these moods," Houston said wistfully while looking in the direction Lexi had gone.

"Yeah, so does Dotty," Jeff said shaking his head in sympathy.

"No. I mean, sometimes she's great," Houston said looking Jeff in the eye.

"So's Dotty," said Jeff with a knowing nod.

"Yeah...What are we gonna do? I know I'm crazy about her and I know she likes me. But how do you live with it, man," Houston asked pleadingly.

Jeff let out a long, loud sigh. "You get used to tuning them out. What is it with females anyway? I really thought she was different. Well, I wish you all the luck, Houston."

Jeff walked out of the solarium. A couple minutes later, Lexi walked back in.

"And another thing..." Lexi said loudly with an I want no argument from you tone.

Houston looked up and started to say something to Lexi but stopped as she barely shook her head and opened her eyes widely. Lexi saw the understanding dawn on Houston's face that Jeff was in hearing range.

"I want to go out for dinner tonight."

Houston stood up in a defensive stance.

"But we've been out almost every night this month. I'm tired, and if we are going shopping today, I'll be beat.

I just want to stay home and relax. Please," Houston said making his voice sound tired and whiny.

"No. I sat home bored last night. I won't do it again. We're going out," Lexi stated forcefully.

Houston sat down and looked up at the ceiling, resting the back of his head on the chair back.

"Okay. It's up to you, Lexi," he said in a totally defeated tone.

"Yes. It should be up to me. I know what's best for us," she purred and sauntered away.

Jeff was back in the room as soon as Lexi's foot fall was no longer audible.

Hiding behind the same plant, she felt like a spy; but she wanted to make sure he bought the entire scene.

"Wow. I thought Dotty was a hard woman. Lexi seems to have her beat. Why don't you cut her loose? You can do better," he said with sincere concern as he looked down at Houston.

"No. I, ahh, I…" Houston looked down, unable to continue. It was obvious how much Houston cared about Lexi.

"Oh man. Houston, didn't I teach you never to fall for a woman? Having one is a necessary evil, but you should never fall for one. It gets too complicated."

"Yes, but it just…happened."

"You poor guy…Well, the infatuation will break someday, hopefully for your sake sooner than later." Jeff smiled, slapped Houston on the leg and left.

Lexi heard him whistling in the hall and knew that Jeff had bought the whole thing. She felt bad for fooling Jeff, but she also knew he would never give up otherwise.

Later that day, Houston waited for the women to get ready to go shopping by reading a magazine. He as well as Lexi and Miranda knew Jeff would be watching, so they needed to make the entire act believable. They talked about the guilty feeling they all had for fooling Jeff. But they all knew it was the only way to get him to behave, and they all made a pact to one day tell Jeff and explain. They wanted to work on him as well as the others to get them to turn to God. They felt he would understand their motives once he found Jesus.

They went to a few local shops and browsed around. Lexi had never seen the local shops before. She had always gone to the city to shop by way of the highway, and that came nowhere near town. She found the local shops had fascinating merchandise and even bought a few knick-knacks and trinkets.

They had so much fun that they forgot about dinner until they were very hungry. They decided to go to a small Italian restaurant that Houston loved. Lexi was fond of Italian food and loved the meal of pasta and salad she chose. Miranda chose a personal pizza and a small glass of wine. Houston had the house specialty, lasagna with thick layers of mushroom, onion, and meat. The heavenly smelling garlic bread made Lexi and Miranda sorry they hadn't chosen the same.

They talked about the pumpkin patch and how it would be fun to bring more kids so Demi had someone to play with there. They all decided that Miranda would be the best person to be in charge of finding kids, and Lexi also wanted them to be children that otherwise would not have gotten to go. She did not want them to miss it while taking children whose families would take them. It felt right.

The more they talked about the outing, the more excited they all became. It would be a wonderful day. Houston told them that after getting the pumpkins, they could go on a hayride, walk through a haunted house, and then gorge themselves on huge caramel apples. They decided to go as soon as possible. Of course, it would have to be a weekend since kids were in school. Miranda had three days to come up with some kids who wouldn't get to go unless they went with them. It was a bit of a challenge, and Lexi could see that Miranda was even more excited about that.

She couldn't believe the warm, glowing feelings she kept getting. It just didn't seem to go away. She had never felt so good in her life. She knew she was feeling that way because of Jesus in her heart. The Holy Spirit made it so that other's happiness was the source of her happiness. She never would have dreamed in a million years that she would feel this way—maybe about money, but not at other's happiness. She felt so good. She just wanted so much to share all that she had, including these good feelings.

"I know I'm waiting on the Lord, but I want to share this happiness with people. I want to make many others happy by doing what God wants me to do. Sometimes I feel I will explode."

"I think he'll tell you soon, Honey. Soon…" Miranda patted her hand.

They left the restaurant and headed back to the country club.

Jeff was packing suitcases into a limo when they pulled up.

"Hey Jeff…off so soon," Lexi asked.

Jeff looked at her warily. A knowing look at Houston was not missed by Lexi. "Yep, I'm heading to Paris for a few months. Dotty's parents rented an apartment there, and she is dying to visit the place. Of course I have to go too…" he rolled his eyes and gave Houston a wink as if to say, "Women," as he stepped into the limo and rolled down the window.

"Well, have fun. Is Lark staying here?" Lexi asked.

"Who can tell? I'm sure she'll be in and out like always. She'll find others to party with I'm sure. And her sister is home from school next week, so…"

And with that, Jeff slapped the roof of the limo, and it pulled away.

Lexi felt a bit relieved, even though she knew she shouldn't. She hated to put on an act; and even knowing that one day she would apologize to Jeff and explain, it didn't sit right with her to have been a part of deceiving him. But for now, she knew it was her only option. She didn't want Jeff having feelings for her that she couldn't and wouldn't return.

Chapter 10

*T*he day was chilly and overcast, a perfect October day to go to the pumpkin patch. It felt like the Halloweens that Lexi had as a child. It was cold enough to be fun but warm enough that they were not shivering. The weather was part of the fun. The clouds that hung overhead didn't seem to threaten rain.

Miranda had outdone herself. She had found fifteen children from a children's protective center and a few foster homes that would not be able to go to a pumpkin patch without them. The children ranged in age from four to twelve years old, and some of the center's staff had volunteered to come along and help.

At first, Lexi was afraid of all the children. She had thought they would pick up four or five. This she had not been prepared for.

Once they were at the pumpkin patch, her fears disappeared almost instantly. The looks on the children's faces were amazing. She soon realized that these children had come from homes that could not keep them. Maybe the parents couldn't afford them or the children may have been battered. An idea started to form in Lexi's mind, but it wasn't solid yet. She was starting to wonder if God intended for her to help children. That was a very interesting idea that was interrupted by Houston.

"Hey Lexi…The kids want to go over to the petting zoo. It's a dollar for a cup of feed, and they can each feed the animals. Want to go along?"

"Sure. Sounds fun," she said, smiling to see the children dancing excitedly as they were handed cups of feed.

Lexi remembered her mother and father taking her to a pumpkin patch when she was a child. Every year, they went to Kregger's pumpkin patch. Mr. Kregger was very old and very wise. Lexi liked him instantly and started calling him Grandpa. The year Mr. Kregger passed away Mrs. Kregger decided to close the pumpkin patch. Lexi never wanted to go to any other pumpkin patch, so the tradition died out after that. She had told Miranda that it made her too sad to go anywhere else. Miranda had understood completely. She created a new tradition; and every October the family had a kid's Halloween party instead. Lexi had loved that.

She couldn't remember how she had gotten so far away from her parents since they were so close when she was young, but she supposed it was a gradual thing that goes unnoticed until one day there is a huge gulf between you and the people you should be closest to. It was a sad thing and one she decided would not happen again.

The children were laughing and squealing with joy as Lexi and Houston walked up to the large pens that held small pigs, rabbits, goats, sheep, and even a pony.

Lexi noticed one boy standing back from the crowd. He looked very sad and detached from the others.

"Houston is that one of ours," she asked with a finger to her lip as she looked at the little boy.

"Yes. He was on the bus. Poor little guy seems so sad," Houston said with a soft expression as he turned to look at the little boy.

Lexi walked over to the boy. He was about four years old. He had a mop of black curls and large, brown eyes. His olive skin was the color Lexi had wished her tanning sessions in her teens had turned her skin.

"Hi there…My name's Lexi. What's yours," Lexi said with a friendly smile as she looked down at him.

The little boy looked at her but said nothing.

"It's okay. You don't have to tell me. It just makes it a little easier to talk. Have you been to the pumpkin patch before?"

With that, large tears rolled down the little boy's face. He didn't make a sound. Lexi's instincts took control. She put her hand on his shoulder and knelt down to be at eye level with him.

"It's okay, honey. I'm sorry if I said something that made you feel bad. I wanted you to have fun today. I didn't want you to feel bad."

The little boy wiped his eyes and looked at Lexi again. "It's okay. I know you're the lady who brought us here. I wanted to come, but it reminds me of my mama," the little boy explained between soft sobs.

Lexi told the little boy about her experiences with Mr. Kregger and how she felt very sad when he was gone and she didn't want to go there anymore.

"They told me my mama is dead. In a car 'cident. Do ya think they're lyin' ta me?"

"Oh, honey, I don't think anyone would lie about that."

The boy started to sob. Lexi noticed the cross he was wearing.

"Honey, listen. Do you believe in Jesus?"

The little boy nodded. "Mama told me all 'bout him."

"So your mama believed in Jesus too, huh?"

The little boy nodded again. "She loved the Lord with all her heart. She a'ways told me that."

"Well, I'm going to tell you something right now. And I want you to listen very carefully. Okay?"

The little boy wiped his eyes and looked intently at Lexi.

"When a Christian dies, they go straight up to Jesus. Your mama is in a beautiful place."

"I want to go there too," the little boy said earnestly.

"Well, someday you will. But did you know that each person has things to learn on the earth that God wants us to know before we go to heaven?"

"Mama told me something like that, but I don't wanna learn. I want my mama," Evan said pleadingly as he looked into Lexi's eyes. Her heart broke at seeing the pain in his eyes. She hugged him and kissed the top of his head.

"You know, I bet your mama wants you to learn as much as you can here so that in heaven you will have a really important job. I bet she has told Jesus many wonderful things about you, and I bet she has told Jesus you will do a good job of learning."

The little boy's eyes widened in surprise.

"Really," he asked in a loud whisper.

"Yes. And we should never want to die until it's our time. God created us for a reason, and he brings us home when it's our time. I bet he felt bad though when he had to take your mama from you, but I bet that's why he has now brought us together. I want us to be very good friends." Lexi said with a gentle smile. "Can I know your name now?"

The little boy looked up at the sky and tapped his finger on his chin, then looked at Lexi with a shy smile. "Evan."

Lexi gave Evan a quick hug and said, "Well, Evan, I'm so very happy to meet you. Like I said, I want us to become good friends. Would you like that?"

Evan smiled a small smile and nodded his head.

"Do you think Mama can see me," Evan asked looking at the sky.

"Maybe she can. We don't know much about the next life except that if we belong to Jesus, we have nothing to fear. You'll see your Mama again. You just have to be patient," Lexi said and thought of seeing her father again.

A sure smile spread across her face. When Evan saw the look on Lexi's face, his own smile broadened.

"I'll try."

"That's all anyone can ask, Evan. We should always try. And when we have a hard time, we need to reach out to other Christians and ask for help," Lexi said, looking into Evan's eyes as she held both his hands.

"Are you a Christian?"

"Yes. You know, I am a Christian," Lexi said confidently with a nod of her head.

Lexi felt warmth glowing inside her that had not been there in a long time. Her admission was a kind of awakening of the side of her that had fallen asleep long ago. She marveled at the things she had just said to Evan. When she looked around, she saw Miranda a short distance away with tears in her eyes. Then Miranda smiled to let her know they were good tears.

"Can I come and live with you?" Evan suddenly asked. "I think Mama and Jesus want me to live with you. Mr. and Mrs. Handlan are grouchy, and they don't talk about Jesus. They tell me that Jesus is a fairy tale. But Jesus is real, right?"

"Yes. Of course he's real." Lexi's head spun with the idea of having Evan in her care. How could he ask something like that of a stranger? Then again, he didn't feel like a stranger to her. He was only a small child. She didn't know how to care for a child. She needed to talk to Houston and Miranda about this. They would help her figure it out. Although why she would, even on some level, even consider the idea was beyond her.

"Well, I've never had a child around, and I know nothing really about kids. I don't think I would make a good mother. But I will always be a phone call away. Okay, Evan?" she asked as she saw the light flicker out in his hopeful eyes.

"Okay." Evan said no more.

Lexi put a finger under his chin and gently lifted his face so she could look into his eyes.

"Evan, I'm not going to just disappear. I want you to visit a lot, and I want you to come for Christmas. We're friends now. So no matter what, I want you in my life, and I will be in yours."

Evan hugged Lexi tightly.

Lexi's heart filled with such a strong feeling of love that she hugged him back.

She felt a closeness to Evan she had never felt with a child before. She imagined it was like the feeling you have with your own child. She wanted to protect him from every hurt and only see him smile.

She watched him as he finally joined in with the others, laughed, and had fun. She watched as Houston took a special interest in Evan also and watched him as he played tag with the children and coached Evan on how to find the special little treats the pumpkin patch had hidden as surprises. He didn't tell him where to look but kept it fun by giving small hints.

The hayride was one of the best parts of the entire day. Lexi and Houston sat together, and Evan sat on Houston's lap. Lexi had an odd feeling of being a family. The feeling was pleasant but strange. She didn't know how she felt about it. Her heart felt a tug when she looked at Evan perched proudly on Houston's lap, but why should she feel this way? It bothered her more than she could admit. Then Evan pointed out birds and deer that were wandering the field, and Lexi forgot her apprehension and enjoyed the ride. They laughed at a deer who watched them intently until they got close and then easily sailed over a fence.

Evan had a good eye and spotted a rabbit family close to the fence where the deer had jumped.

"I'd love to have a baby bunny," Evan exclaimed with a large smile on his face.

"But those are wild, and they would be afraid to be away from their mother," Houston said gently.

"Yeah, the babies need to stay with the mommy. That's how God wants it."

Lexi felt tears come to her eyes. Poor little Evan, losing his mother so young, Lexi thought. It made her feel sad until Evan let out a big laugh that got her laughing also.

"What's so funny," Lexi asked wanting to know what was amusing Evan so greatly.

"Look over there," said Houston pointing at a deer with a rabbit chasing it.

The three of them laughed until their sides hurt. It was a fun day, and Lexi wanted it to last forever.

When it was time to go, the children all gathered around Lexi. In one big voice, they shouted, "Thank you, Miss Lexi. We had a lot of fun."

Lexi giggled at their happiness. It made her feel happier than she could remember.

"You're very welcome, children. I want to invite you all to the country club where I'm staying. They have a Halloween movie to play for you that I picked out myself. Also some hot apple cider with real cinnamon sticks."

Lexi laughed as the children all roared with happiness. Lexi caught a glimpse of Houston watching her with an odd look on his face. She caught up with him once the children were all on the bus.

"I didn't get to see much of you today," she said a little sadly.

"I saw a lot of you," Houston answered with a small smile. "You're a very beautiful woman, Lexi Hunter. I never saw anyone light up so much as you did today with the children. I also saw you talking to Evan. He sure is a special kid."

"Yeah, he really is, and so are all the kids. I guess I just saw how children really are for the first time. They're so innocent really and full of mischief. I felt like a kid again. I hadn't realized how old I've been feeling."

"I hear you. It was a lot of fun for me too, Lexi. I haven't had much fun for many years. You brought it all back, and I want to thank you for that." Houston said taking Lexi in his arms and kissing her softly.

Lexi and Houston laughed as the children made noises when they saw the kiss.

At the country club, after the children had all left, Lexi and Houston settled down in front of the fireplace. Miranda excused herself. She wanted to take a shower after the long but fun day with the children.

"Lexi…"

Houston hesitated so long Lexi knew he was having a hard time.

"What is it, Houston? You can tell me anything."

"I know…I mean…I feel like I can, which is such a good feeling. It's just…I want to say this the right way. I don't want to mess it up." Houston looked into Lexi's eyes briefly, than stared at the floor. She could see his jaw working as he ground his teeth.

"Just say it. It'll be all right." Lexi smiled reassuringly at him when he glanced back at her.

"Lexi, I'm in love with you. I've been in love with you for a very long time. I love being with you. The more we're together the more I want to be with you."

Lexi looked at him intently. Her heart beat quickened as did her breath.

"I guess I want to know how you feel…about me."

Lexi looked into the fire and thought for a moment.

"I really wasn't a hundred percent sure until I saw you with Evan today. I realized that I, too, am in love with you. I can't imagine ever being without you. And the times that you're not with me I spend waiting for you to get here. I miss you when we aren't together." Lexi reached up and stroked Houston's cheek lovingly.

Houston stood up and took Lexi's hand. He led her to a stool next to the fireplace and sat her down. He got down on one knee. Lexi's heart beat very fast. He reached into his pocket and produced a small, blue, velvet box with a ribbon on it. He handed it to Lexi.

As she looked at the box, her eyes mysteriously filled with tears, making it hard to see. When she opened the box, Houston said clearly, "Be my wife, Lexi. I promise you I will do everything in my power to make every day a trip to the pumpkin patch."

Lexi laughed and said, "Yes! Oh, Houston, you have made me the happiest woman in the world."

Houston jumped up and grabbed Lexi. He easily picked her up and swung her around as he hugged her closely to him. He stopped turning, and they kissed a deep, loving kiss that made Lexi's heart feel it would burst with all the love she felt for this man who was to be her husband.

"You're going to be my husband," Lexi said in a tone of wonder.

"Yes, that happens when you marry a guy," Houston teased with a happy smile.

"Oh, Houston, I don't deserve all this happiness."

"Yes you do, Lexi. What you did for those kids today and what you have done for me…there are no words." Houston's eyes misted.

"Houston, you deserve to be happy too. People make mistakes. You were a kid. You need to forgive yourself and know that God has forgiven you. I'm so happy right now. I never thought it was possible to be this happy. I thought millions of dollars and beautiful things would make me happy, but I ended up feeling so empty. It's God and love that have brought me to this place in my life. But he has also blessed me with all this so that I can be a blessing to others," Lexi said as she thought about all she had.

"And you are," Houston said smoothing her hair and then softly rubbing his thumb against her cheek.

"I want to be more though, more of a blessing. I want to do something to help people, children. I know I need to help children. Just how I do it…that's what I'm not sure of…"

"Lexi, that's awesome. I love kids," Houston said, his face lighting with excitement.

"Evan asked me if he could come and live with me," Lexi said cautiously, uncertainty on her face.

"You're kidding. He asked me that too. Well, actually, he asked me if he could live with me and Miss Lexi," Houston said with a grin. Lexi sighed with relief. She should have known Houston would like the idea.

"Really? That little one is so smart." Lexi shook her head and laughed.

"Yeah, he knew we should be together. I didn't tell him. He just knew. After we're married, let's talk about Evan. I really would love to have him be part of our family."

"Oh, Houston, I feel exactly the same way."

Lexi threw her arms around him, and they kissed deeply. She had come to the realization that Evan was meant to be with them. She no longer feared being a bad mother. She loved Houston, and she loved Evan. That was what mattered. Miranda was there to help her along the way. She would also pray about being a good mother, and she knew that trusting Jesus would be the entire backbone to her family's happiness.

Miranda cleared her throat as she walked back out into the living room where Lexi and Houston stood.

"You two better cool it. Intruding company," Miranda teased.

"Mom, have we got news for you."

Lexi told her everything, and Miranda was so happy she cried happy tears. Twice in one day. It made everything perfect.

Chapter 11

*L*exi and Houston decided to have a Christmas wedding. They wanted a small wedding, and all the staff would be back the first week of November.

They found out at their second visit with Appel that she would be out by then, and she was overjoyed to be asked to be Lexi's maid of honor.

When everyone was back at Rivenwood, all refreshed from their vacations, Lexi called everyone into the great room and told them all the news. They were all very pleased and let Houston know he would be a very welcome addition to the household.

Lexi asked Tabitha and Burdia to be her bridesmaids. They were all very excited, especially Burdia, who also, out of character, was very shy when asking if Lexi had a wedding planner.

"I believe so. I'm hoping that you will be my wedding planner."

Burdia's eyes got as big as saucers, and they misted as her face broke into the widest smile Lexi had ever seen on Burdia's face.

"Thank you, Mistress. I'll make your day a dream come true."

"I know you will. That's why I wouldn't even dream of having anyone else," Lexi said as she kissed Burdia's cheek.

With all the hustle and bustle of getting ready for the wedding, time flew and it was almost Thanksgiving. Lexi had never dreamed there was so much to do. Burdia would appear when something needed to be done. Then she would be out of sight again. True to her word, Burdia was making the wedding a dream come true. She knew Lexi and Houston's favorite colors and had used shades of silver and blue that looked beautiful together. She got Lexi's approval on every little detail, but Lexi knew that Burdia had a gift for organizing and she also had the most wonderful taste. There was nothing that Burdia brought to Lexi and Houston that they did not love.

Thanksgiving at Rivenwood Manor that year was so different from the two before. Everyone was involved in decorating the mansion in all kinds of festive autumn décor with life-sized pilgrim and Indian cutouts, tables filled with delicious food and fruit juice drink, and even some stuffed squirrel and chipmunk toys here and there to add to the fun.

Everyone arose early Thanksgiving morning and went to church, each to their own. Lexi felt good to know that all the people she now had in her world were Christians.

The service that Lexi, Houston, and Miranda attended was given by a new, young minister they had never seen before. The passion and confidence with which he spoke made the service one of the most inspiring Lexi had ever attended. They all shook hands with Pastor Kendal as they left and thanked him for such a wonderful service.

They arrived home after the staff, as their church was farthest away. The smells that greeted them as they walked in the door made them instantly hungry. Lexi and Miranda went upstairs to change, and Houston sat in an overstuffed chair next to the fire in the great room.

Tabitha's sister, Abbey, had been moved into the main house and was given a suite on the second floor. She had gone into remission, and her prognosis was looking good. Doctors said it was the level of care she was getting that did it. Lexi felt sad that she wasn't getting as good of care when she was on public insurance, but she knew that the ways of the world were usually painful and unjust. She felt happy that Abbey was improving. It did a lot for Demi's spirits to be able to play with his mom again.

This made Lexi think of poor little Evan. He was such a sweet, loving child. It broke her heart to think of him missing his mom and feeling out of place with his foster parents. The thought was interrupted by Miranda knocking on her door.

"Well, dear, are you ready to stuff yourself?" she asked with a huge grin.

"I don't know if I'm ready, but I know I will do just that," she said with a laugh.

Lexi and Miranda made their way to the dining room.

When the table was set for dinner and the food was prepared, Lexi summoned the staff to gather in the dining room.

"Friends, I wish for you all to join us. This is a time of thanking our Lord for all he has given us, and I want us to all do that together. I am so thankful to have such wonderful people around me who cared for me even when what I deserved was a slap upside the head. I now consider you not only friends but family."

"That explains all the extra place settings," Raymond mused out loud and Reeves chuckled.

"You are spoilin' us, Miss Lexi." Tabitha giggled.

"No, Tabby. I should have done this last year and the year before. As long as it's not awkward for any of you, that is."

They all said it was not, and they sat down to a wonderful dinner. They took turns giving heartfelt thanks to God.

Chris had outdone himself. He told them he had missed cooking and had put all his effort into the meal.

"You truly succeeded with this meal. It's the best I've ever had," Lexi said and wondered how that statement could be true every time she said it, but it was.

Chris's face turned a dark red, but his eyes showed how happy her statement had made him. He had been hoping he did a good job.

After dinner, they all played a few games and then retired to the great room, where the large stone fireplace was blazing and heating the room nicely.

It was the best Thanksgiving Lexi had since she was with her mother and father at home. She felt a pang of intense grief as she thought about how very much she wished her dad and Aunt Cami were there with them.

Even though she hadn't known her very well, Aunt Cami had brought all this happiness to Lexi. She also had been able to read Lexi well enough to know that one day she would do the right thing with all her blessings.

Lexi sat by the fire on a small pillow next to Abbey.

"Yer the kindest person I've ever known," Abbey said with gratitude.

"Well, Abbey, I can't take the credit. God opened my eyes a few months ago. And when I saw what I'd become, I couldn't stomach it. I was so ashamed of myself. And then he taught me how to not only feel better about myself in spite of the things I had done in the past but also how to spread the blessing he had given me around. I remember seeing a saying once about how you can't receive more blessings from God if you don't share the ones he has already given you, like, if your hands are full; you have no room to accept more. I didn't think anything of it at the time, but now I know what it meant. And it isn't that I want more blessings for myself but that I want more to share with others. That's the best part of it all. I want to help others. I want to be a part of making other's lives easier and happier. It feels so good. It's the most amazing feeling I've ever felt."

"Yes," Abbey said with an excited nod. "I remember sharing a small turkey with our postal man a few years ago. He had nowhere to go and we didn't have much, but it somehow was enough. And it was so much fun. I guess that no matter what we have, how much or how little, we can always share our blessings and God provides enough."

"You're so right about that." Lexi smiled and gave Abbey a quick hug. She liked Abbey very much. Abbey had strength in her that Lexi admired.

Houston sat down next to Lexi.

"Can I intrude on your conversation," he asked with a friendly grin.

"Course…I'm really sleepy after that large meal. Think I will take my leave," Abbey said with a smile and large yawn.

"Sounds good…Have a good nap," Lexi said as Abbey got to her feet and walked out of the great room.

"She sure is something, so strong," Lexi said as she watched Abbey leave the room.

"I know another who's as strong." Houston rubbed her back softly.

"Me? No. I don't think I could go through what she has and survive," Lexi said shaking her head and looking at the floor.

"Yes, you could. I know you. You have that inner strength," Houston said as he gently lifted Lexi's chin so that her eyes met his.

Lexi stroked his cheek, then leaned in and gave him a soft kiss.

"You know, I guess you're right because that inner strength comes from faith. I never thought I would be talking and believing the way I do now. It all really comes together once you take it all seriously," Lexi said looking around the room at all the wonderful people in her life. She smiled warmly.

"Yes. I know if I hadn't had my faith I wouldn't have survived after the accident. It kept me going when no one wanted me around. I knew that Jesus still cared, he still loved me even when the world seemed to turn its back on me," Houston said pushing a lock of hair away from Lexi's face. Lexi looked into his eyes.

"How did you know? I mean, I know what you're saying is true. I'm just curious," Lexi asked with her head tilted slightly.

Houston looked up toward the ceiling in thought. After a moment he looked back at Lexi. She saw tears in his eye but his face was full of peace.

"I could feel him like I never have before. He even gave me a vision of my house in heaven. I know it might sound silly, but he did. I just closed my eyes and saw it.

And I felt so at peace. Since then, I've done my best to please him. Not because I'm trying to earn my place in heaven. That would be impossible. But I want to please him for all he has done for me. You know?"

Lexi nodded with a lopsided grin.

"I do know. That's part of the reason it's driving me crazy to know exactly what he wants me to do with all this money he's given me. I want to please him with what I do. I don't want to let him down."

Houston laughed lightly.

"He'll let you know when the time's right."

"I know. I just hope I'm smart enough to understand what he's saying to me," Lexi said folding her arms over her chest and making a goofy frown.

"My little Lexi, you'll know. You'll know," Houston said as he cradled Lexi in his arms.

The day was winding down, and everyone seemed to be very comfortable sitting in the great room, chatting. Chris got up and disappeared for about half an hour.

Just after Abbey came back downstairs, Chris rolled in a pastry cart filled with all kinds of delicacies. Abbey squealed with delight over finding a peach turnover. She had mentioned a few days before how much she loved the ones her mother made but could only find apple and cherry at the market. Lexi saw the glint in Chris's eyes and realized he was a bit smitten with Abbey.

Lexi saw the exchanged glances between Chris and Abbey and saw that the feeling was mutual. It was wonderful to see Abbey so happy. She prayed that Jesus would bring Abbey and Chris together if that was his will. They would be a wonderful couple, and she had seen Chris play with Demi. They spent time doing things together the way a father would with his son. Lexi realized she had not noticed these things on a very deep level. But she made it a point to start praying for all of her household to have many blessings and for their safety.

After everyone had retired for the evening, Lexi and Houston stood out on the back patio where they had first had lunch together. They stood holding each other and watching the waves in the moonlight.

"You've made a lot of people very happy today. You gave them something that can never be taken away."

"What's that?"

"Love…And you gave them family. You turned this into a real Thanksgiving for everyone. My parents are always gone on Thanksgiving. This is the first real one I've ever had. How I adore you, my wife-to-be."

Lexi giggled. "You make me very happy too, Houston."

"Lexi, I want to talk to you about something," Houston said hesitantly.

"What is it," Lexi ask anxiously. She looked up into Houston's eyes.

"I want to talk about Evan. I felt very strongly that he should have been here today," Houston said then looked at Lexi.

"Really? I had the same feeling but didn't know how you would take that." Lexi backed away from Houston a few steps and took his hands.

"I believe he belongs with us. Ever since the pumpkin patch, I have missed him greatly."

Lexi let go of his hands and grabbed his biceps tightly. "So have I!"

"So we are agreed? We both want to bring him home and raise him?" Houston grinned widely leaning down slightly to be closer to Lexi's face.

"Yes!"

Houston grabbed Lexi and spun her around.

"Monday morning, we'll go get things started," Houston said after setting Lexi on her feet again. He rubbed his chin and looked unseeingly around.

"Oh, Houston…Just when I think I am the happiest I can ever be, you spring something else wonderful on me!"

"I intend to do that for the rest of our life."

Lexi pulled Houston's face down to hers and kissed him deeply.

Lexi was on top of the world. She knew she was a very blessed person, and she thanked God for it over and over. Nothing could take her happiness away, she was sure of it.

Lexi roused out of a deep sleep. She was a hard sleeper, so waking took a great effort. She knew it was the middle of the night as the room was pitch black. She wondered what had awakened her, and then the phone rang again. Who in the world could be calling at this time of night?

It was Houston. He had called the foster home to talk to Evan and had found out he was no longer there. He was in the hospital. Then the woman had hung up. No further explanation. Houston had called everyone he could think of trying to get information before calling Lexi, which was why it was so late, but had only run into dead-ends.

Lexi called around until she found out what hospital Evan was in. She feigned being his aunt. She and Houston were on their way to the hospital within a half hour of Houston's call.

Lexi was shaking. She knew something was very wrong. Why would the woman not offer any kind of explanation? And when Lexi had called the woman to demand an explanation, there was no answer. It was all too strange.

When they arrived at the hospital, the nurse did not buy Lexi's story of being Evan's aunt. Houston contacted Mr. Sutton, and he was able to help them gain access to Evan once he found out their intentions to adopt Evan.

Lexi and Houston were just about to walk into Evan's room when a doctor stopped them.

"Mr. Cheyenne, Miss Hunter, may I speak to you before you go in," the doctor asked with an obvious amount of concern.

Lexi started to shake again.

"Certainly," Houston said and guided Lexi to a chair in the room the doctor indicated.

"I understand you are looking to adopt Evan."

"Yes," Lexi said quickly.

"Have you any idea why Evan is with us?"

"No. We don't know anything yet," Houston said with a sick look on his face.

"It seems his foster father came home and found some finger paint on the carpet in Evan's room. He beat Evan unconscious. He has not regain consciousness since being brought in last night."

Lexi felt tears fall from her eyes, and then the sobs came. Houston put his arms around her and held her tight.

"Money is no object. I want all the best people on his case," Houston said shakily.

"Of course, Mr. Cheyenne...I will contact several experts and get them here as soon as possible. Before you go in to see Even, please understand that he barely resembles the little boy you know. There is considerable swelling."

"The foster father, where is he?" demanded Lexi as she wiped her nose with a tissue the doctor offered.

"I believe he's in jail, unless his family was able to bail him out. I do know he was arrested though."

"What a monster," Lexi said quietly, resolving to never let Evan near people like those foster parents again.

Lexi and Houston walked slowly to Evan's room and opened the door. Part of Evan's head was bandaged, but the part of his face that showed was indeed swollen. He didn't look like Evan at all. There were tubes in his nose and in his mouth, and there were wires coming from all over his tiny body. Lexi's heart fell.

She gingerly took Evan's hand and kissed it.

"Evan, honey, it's Lexi. Houston and I are here. And we will never leave you again. Honey, you have to get better. Houston and I want to be your mommy and daddy. Oh, baby, please get better." Lexi cried great sobs.

Houston's own tears ran freely down his cheeks.

They sat with Evan until the specialists arrived, and they asked Lexi and Houston to wait in the waiting room. Time dragged. Then they saw Evan being taken from his room.

"What—?" Lexi started.

"We're taking Evan for another MRI, among other testing. We want to know exactly what we're dealing with," a tall, thin, older man said.

"Oh," Lexi said and she returned to her seat in the waiting room.

When Houston sat beside her, Lexi pounded her legs with her fits.

"Why didn't we get him out of there sooner?"

"Lexi, we didn't know this would happen."

"But he wanted me to help him, to protect him. I know that now, and I just ignored it like I did my father's sickness. Houston, I'm a monster."

"Lexi, that's not true. Honey, you're upset. I feel horrible guilt that I didn't say something sooner about adopting Evan also, but we didn't know. We just didn't know."

Lexi fell into Houston's arms and sobbed uncontrollably.

Time crawled even slower. Lexi fell into an exhausted sleep in Houston's arms until Houston nudged her gently. Lexi shot up to her feet when she saw the doctors coming toward them.

"What have you found? Is he going to be all right? What can be done?" Lexi begged.

The tall, thin doctor introduced himself as Samuel Stephens. He asked Lexi and Houston to follow him to a consultation room.

Once they were all seated, Dr. Stephens started.

"The boy has had severe blunt trauma to the head. There is bleeding on his brain, and he has been unconscious for longer than we would like. Luckily, there are some very good doctors at this facility, and they knew to drain the blood to relieve the pressure to minimize the chance of brain damage. However, being that…Evan," Dr. Stephens said after looking at his paperwork, "has not regained consciousness…we can only wait until that happens to assess any damage that might have occurred. He's stable. He was stable when we got here. Where we will come in is when he regains consciousness. All we can do for now is…wait."

"We can also pray," said Houston.

He and Lexi went to the chapel. Lexi prayed harder than she had ever prayed in her life. She prayed for a miracle for this little one, for God to heal him quickly. She let him know she was ready to do whatever he wanted her to do no matter what it was.

A thought flashed into her mind, many kids were in the same situation as Evan. They were in abusive foster homes. She knew there were a lot of good people who ran foster homes but that there were also bad ones. She suddenly knew what God was telling her. She took Houston's hand and led him to the hallway.

"Houston, the house, the money, it's all to take care of the children."

"Huh? What children?"

"Children like Evan, little ones who need a safe place. That's what God wants me to do with the money and the house."

"You're sure?"

"Yes. I have no doubts."

"Then that's what we'll do."

"I'll get a hold of Mr. Sutton in the morning and find out all the legal stuff first. I'll find out exactly what we need in place to get this moving as soon as possible."

Lexi was filled with excitement. Now she knew the reason God had given her the money, and she knew that Evan would pull through. She had felt Jesus's hand on hers as she prayed. She was sure of it.

"I also know Evan is going to be okay."

"Yes. I felt Jesus's presence also. And instantly, my fears were gone."

"Let's go sit with our son." Lexi smiled.

Chapter 12

*T*hree days later, Lexi and Houston were worn out from their ever-present vigil over Evan. He had not regained consciousness, and the doctors were becoming pessimistic. Lexi refused to hear their prognosis or opinions. She kept telling them that the Lord would heal Evan in his time, not theirs. Lexi could see in Houston's eyes that he was beginning to fear that she was building something up in her own mind that would devastate her. He confirmed it when he decided they needed to talk.

"Honey, I know how much you want Evan to wake up—."

"And he will. I have faith."

"But what if it's his time?"

"Houston, I felt Jesus tell me that Evan would be okay right here in this hospital. I felt it so strongly, and I have not doubted ever since. I won't doubt it. Jesus can do anything. He raised people from the dead. He'll bring our son back."

"But—."

"No buts, Houston. This is something I'm sure of. You'll see. He's just waiting for the right time, and I wait patiently for that time too. It's also a time of testing for us. Mom told me that God does that. He doesn't answer some prayers right away because it doesn't strengthen our faith. But it doesn't mean that he isn't going to answer them. And it doesn't mean that Evan will be hurt by the waiting either. It doesn't matter what doctors say. Jesus is so very much more powerful and wise than they are."

"Okay. I just want you to be all right."

"I am. Mr. Sutton is working on all the details for us to start taking in children, and the workers are busy getting thing ready at Rivenwood. I know that the first child to come home to us will be Evan. And all our foster children will play with him when they come to stay with us also."

"I want that too. I want Evan home for our wedding. Do you think we should postpone it?"

"No. I have faith Evan will be coming home with us in plenty of time."

Lexi smiled, and Houston believed her.

They walked hand in hand back to Evan's room. Lexi sat in the chair next to Evan's bed and took his little hand in hers and kissed it. Houston bent down and kissed the top of Lexi's head and then also kissed Evan's little head.

Suddenly Lexi's face lit up and she said, "Houston, Evan just squeezed my hand!"

They both looked at Evan's face, and his eyes fluttered open.

"I had a dream," Evan started out with a scratchy voice as he looked at Lexi.

Houston gave him a sip of water and went to call the doctors in.

"He said you are now my mommy and Houston is my daddy. It was a nice dream." Evan smiled tiredly. He closed his eye for a moment and then looked again at Lexi.

"Oh, honey, we are. You're coming home with us. We're adopting you," Lexi squeezed Evan's little hand then leaned down and kissed his cheek.

"Really? Did Jesus really talk to me?" Evan tried to sit up but Lexi gently held him down and smiled.

"I bet he did," she said as she rubbed his arm lovingly.

"Is it Christmas," Evan asked squinting and smiling as if confused.

"No. Christmas isn't for a few weeks yet. Why," Lexi ask taking his hand into both of hers, her heart racing.

"I 'ready got my present," Evan said with a large grin.

Lexi let out her breath as she realized Evan was Okay. Then her eyes welled up, and she kissed Evan's hand.

The doctors had Lexi and Houston leave the room so they could examine Evan.

Lexi and Houston went to the waiting room and made more plans. Lexi was sure Evan would be coming home soon, and they wanted to do as much as they could to make their son's life as wonderful as they could. They made plans to do a family Christmas tree trek at a tree farm to get their tree and to go on a sleigh ride with lots of hot chocolate in tow. They talked and planned about all the wonderful things they could do with Evan as long as the doctors approved their plans.

A few hours later, the doctors came to the waiting room with perplexed looks on their faces.

"What is it?" Lexi asked guardedly.

"That little boy has an incredible will to live. His body has just about totally healed, and we find no evidence of brain damage at all. Of course, we want to keep him a few more days and run some extensive tests. But if all turns out okay, you should be able to take him home this weekend," Dr. Stephens said, looking like he couldn't believe his own words.

"Thank you so much, Doctor," Houston said as he pumped the doctor's hand.

The test showed no permanent damage, and Evan was almost as good as new when he left the hospital with his new mom and dad. Lexi was very happy when the swelling went down and the bandages were removed. Evan soon looked like the little boy she had fallen in love with. Both Lexi and Houston kept tearing up when he called them Mommy and Daddy.

The doctors approved Evan being able to go places as long as he was not fatigued. Lexi and Houston took extra special care of their son. They brought a padded wagon for Evan to ride in when they went looking for their tree. A week later, when they went on a sleigh ride through the snowy mountain, they brought plenty of hot chocolate to drink to keep them warm. Evan sat on Houston's lap under a thick quilt. His eyes shone with the love he was receiving and the happiness he felt.

Lexi and Houston laughed almost constantly at Evan's jokes. They complained with grins about their faces hurting from smiling so much. Evan complained about them kissing all the time, only to ask them if they were going to kiss already when they hadn't in a while. Those times, Houston took Lexi in his arms and kissed her, then danced her around.

Miranda was, of course, the doting grandmother. She read Evan and Demi bedtime stories in the great room, and then helped tuck them each in at bedtime.

Evan's bedroom was a little boy's dream but was not overdone. Lexi and Houston knew that spoiling a child was not God's way. But they also made sure he was happy with it. He had a racecar bed and a modest toy box filled with appropriate toys for a four-year-old. Evan was a very happy little boy. He constantly thanked Lexi and Houston for everything, which made them a little sad but also made them happy that he realized that the world didn't just hand you things normally. They also reminded him to thank God for everything he was blessed with. His answer was always the same: "I 'ready did." He would say it with such a sweet smile that it made them ashamed of how they often forgot to thank God for all their blessings, but it also encouraged them to remember to do just that more often.

It was wonderful having a son who understood things the way Evan did. Lexi and Houston marveled at the way he accepted things so quickly and adjusted to changes. His birth mother had taught him very well about God and had nurtured his faith constantly. It was Evan who suggested they have after-dinner Bible reading by the fire. Lexi, Houston, and Miranda loved the idea; and soon, they were having the household come to the great room to join in. They waited until everyone was done with their nightly duties.

They had their devotional times at about 7:00 p.m. for an hour, all taking turns reading a favorite passage or someone picking one for that night; and then they would discuss what was read.

One night, they got into a particularly fascinating discussion as Abbey chose the miracle of feeding the five thousand. Each person had an experience that related to that miracle and shared it. They ended up talking for hours. It was an exhilarating night, and they all went to bed with many prayers of thanks to God.

Houston had moved into the cottage since he was spending so much time at Rivenwood, so the late devotional nights were fine for everyone; and no one wanted to miss one.

Lexi also suspected that he had taken her advice and talked to his parents and things had not gone well. She didn't question him as she knew he would confide in her when the time was right for him.

Chapter 13

*T*ime seemed to go by in a blink, and Lexi was preparing to go to the church on her wedding day. Everyone was excited. Miranda had come to tell Lexi about fifty times how much she loved her and how exited she was for her. She also couldn't get over how beautiful Lexi looked. Miranda said she looked like a china doll, very delicate and petite.

Lexi shooed her away, but she loved the attention. Her nerves were brittle, and she knew she would trip walking down the aisle.

Evan was with Houston, getting ready. He was the ring-bearer. Lexi saw the pride in his eyes and in his stance when she and Houston asked him. He said he would love to. Lexi felt such a surge of love for her son when he acted so grownup. He was a miracle and a blessing to her and Houston.

Before too long a time had passed, Lexi was ready. Burdia went to tell the organist. Once the music started playing, Lexi walked out to meet Reeves, who would walk her down the aisle. Lexi could see the warmth in his eyes. He was a true friend, and Lexi loved him very much. She had grown to love all her staff.

She took Reeves's arm, and he guided her down the aisle to Houston without a trip or a pause all the way. She leaned heavily on his arm, but he seemed to support her effortlessly.

At the altar, Reeves took her hand and placed it on Houston's arm. Houston looked deeply into Lexi's eyes. The love she saw there made her catch her breath. His face was very serious. She knew he considered this ceremony to be very serious. It was something he would hold in his heart forever.

They turned to the minister, and the ceremony began. It all seemed to go by in a blink and Lexi was kissing her new husband. She got so caught up in the flurry of cheers, hugs, and kisses that she picked up Evan and twirled him around. Then she kissed him soundly on the cheek.

Houston grabbed on to both of them and kissed and hugged them over and over. They all started laughing and hugging.

The reception was beautiful, a lot of well-wishes and wonderful speeches all caught on tape so that Houston and Lexi could watch it again one day, probably more than once.

They danced to Lexi's favorite song, which became her and Houston's song. Lexi danced with Evan numerous times. He had blossomed into a real little gentleman. He was such a good-natured and good-tempered little boy. He was also very aware of other's feelings. Lexi was so happy that God had chosen her and Houston to raise him. She thanked God every day for her family and prayed for their safety and strength.

There was no alcohol at the reception due to Lexi and Houston's wishes. The food and different fruity drinks filled everyone; and by midnight, everyone was ready to call it a night.

Lexi and Houston ran down a path to their limo where the well-wishers tossed bird seed at them. They all got into their own cars to head home.

Lexi and Houston decided their honeymoon would be spent at home, as neither wanted to leave their family. They sequestered themselves in their suite. They were not seen for one week, during which time they grew closer than ever. The physical intimacy changed the love they had for each other into something so very much deeper and stronger. Lexi was a virgin not because of God, as she had run far away from him by her high school and college days, but because her pursuit of money had been all-encompassing. Now she thanked God for keeping her from doing something that would have taken away from this special time with Houston.

When Lexi and Houston rejoined the rest of the household a week later, they were a very strong and united front. The love they had for each other shone in their eyes as they looked at each other or spoke to each other. Everyone could see it and thanked God that their mistress was so happy and in love.

Chapter 14

*L*ife settled into a wonderful routine that included a lot of hugs, kisses, and Bible study. Work was going well with adding walls to accommodate more children. Mr. Sutton had worked everything out so that Lexi and Houston could take in up to ten children at any one time. They hired a nurse, two special teachers, and a counselor who was specially trained to help young children who had been abused or abandoned.

When the children started to arrive, Rivenwood was ready for them. The house seemed to burst at the seams with all the love and happiness. There were trying times; but with God being a part of every part of Rivenwood, they were able to get through them and look forward to the future.

One day, Lexi knocked on her mother's bedroom door.

"Come in."

Lexi opened the door and found Miranda sitting in a well-padded lounge chair that was facing a huge window overlooking the ocean. Miranda looked very content and comfortable.

"Hello dear…"

"Hi Mom…I was walking in the rose garden and realized something. I wanted to share it with you. I know you probably already know what I'm about to say, but I want you to know that I know it now too."

Miranda smiled happily. "What is it, my sweet daughter?"

Lexi pulled another chair over to her mother's and sat down facing her.

"I've come to realize that when I wanted wealth, when I strove to achieve financial security, when I pampered myself shamelessly, and when I began drinking and doing such unchristian things—"

"It's in the past, my Lexi," Miranda said, patting Lexi's hand lovingly when Lexi hesitated.

"I know, Mom. But I've finally realized why," Lexi said, looking into her mother's eyes.

"I see. Okay. Why?"

"I was always trying to fill this emptiness inside myself, this void that hurt. The pain drove me to be selfish. It drove me to ignore what God was telling me and what you were telling me. Unless Jesus lives inside you, that void can drive you to do any kind of horrible thing. It eats away at you, and you'll end up doing anything to fill it. I now understand humans a bit better. All the horrible things they do are a way of trying to fill that emptiness. Spending money fills it, but only temporarily. And I suppose sex, drugs, and all the rest fill it, but always temporarily. It's only once you have Jesus living inside you to fill that void that the void is really and permanently filled. I feel whole and complete now. I don't need anything but him now to make me feel good, and the pain is totally gone."

Lexi relaxed and sat back in her chair.

Miranda beamed. "Yes, you've made a very important revelation. I never thought about that, but I know that what you're saying is true," she said sitting forward with her hands clasped.

Lexi leaned forward and took Miranda's hands in hers.

"Mom...thank you for praying for me. And thank you for not giving up on me for all those years. I know now that if it wasn't for you, I might have been lost. I know now how powerful prayer really is."

They hugged and enjoyed the rest of the afternoon together.

Epilogue

"Raymond, have you seen the angel for the top of the tree?" Houston asked as Raymond came into the great room.

"Why yes. I put it in a special place to keep it dry and in good condition," Raymond said and turned to get the angel.

"Good thinking," said Houston as he turned back to help Lexi and the children put more ornaments on the tree.

There was a large fire burning in the fireplace. Miranda and Abbey sat on the sofa near it, making plans for the party the next night as they sipped hot apple cider.

Reesa, Lexi and Houston's daughter, toddled over to the tree and let out a loud cry as she touched the tree. Ten-year-old Evan put the bulb he was holding down and ran to his little sister. He picked her up and kissed her finger. Reesa rewarded him with a large smile as left over tears rolled down her face. Evan brushed them off her checks.

"Reesie, want a cookie?" Evan asked as he bounced her on his hip.

"Rees coo! Rees coo," said Reesa in baby talk, clapping her hands.

Lexi had stopped trimming the tree to watch her son and daughter with pride. Houston came up behind her and put his arms around her waist.

"We have been so very blessed with our children," Lexi said, leaning back into Houston's chest and caressing his arms with her hands.

"Yes, we have." Houston kissed the top of Lexi's head.

"Hey, love birds," said Tad. "Soph and me can't decorate this big ol' tree by ourselves!"

Lexi and Houston laughed as they turned back to the tree where their other children were busy trimming the tree.

Tad was a very sweet eleven year old whose face had a deep scar from his left eye to his chin. It had happened in the car accident that had claimed his mother's and father's lives. He was a baby at the time of the accident and didn't remember his parents. He had lived with an elderly aunt until she was no longer able to care for him. Mr. Sutton informed Lexi and Houston of Tad's situation, and they became foster parents for him when he was nine. It was a perfect fit and little time passed before Lexi and Houston adopted Tad.

Sophie had joined the family a year later. She had been eight when her mother abandoned her at the center. Sophie was very shy at first, but when Lexi and Houston brought Reesa home from the hospital, Sophie became a second doting mom. Lexi nicknamed Sophie My China Doll because of her shiny blonde curls and crystal blue eyes. They adopted Sophie as soon as the law allowed it.

"Well, now, are ya ready for refreshments?" asked Tabitha as she wheeled in a cart with more mugs of hot apple cider and a platter of Christmas cookies.

The children all ran to the cart with cheers and took turns getting mugs and cookies.

Lexi and Houston held hands as they walked over to Tabitha.

"You timed that perfectly," said Houston with a warm smile.

"I thought it would suit well as ya've all been working so hard to get things just right fer tomorrow night," Tabitha said with a wink.

"Well, you've done a wonderful job, getting this place into the spirit of Christmas," said Lexi as she hugged Tabitha. "I just love this time of year!"

"Me too," said Tabitha with a squeal. Lexi and Houston laughed.

They ate and drank till they were satisfied, then finished trimming the tree. It had been a very good day.

The next afternoon, Lexi walked through the house making sure everything was just right. She and Houston had invited their old friends from their party days over for a Christmas party.

The only one who could not make it was Lark Winston. She had followed in her father's footsteps and become the head of his corporation. She had given up her party life, but was now as addicted to working as she had been to partying. It was sad, but all attempts Lexi and Houston had made to reach her had failed. But they continued to pray for her salvation every day.

Lexi went through the house, lighting the pine and cinnamon scented candles. Houston had a fire going in the great room and had hung mistletoe in every doorway of the first floor. They met back in the entry doorway to the great room.

"Perfect," Lexi said as she grabbed Houston and pulled him down for a kiss. Houston put his arms around her and lifted her off her feet, kissing her back lovingly.

"They're at it again," said Tad to the other children. He rolled his eyes playfully as the children came up to the door way.

"Yep, we sure are," said Houston as he hugged Lexi tightly and set her back on her feet. "We will be at it for the rest of our lives."

"That's good," said Evan with a peaceful smile. "I'm glad our family will always be together."

Lexi hugged Evan and kissed his check, "Me too, honey."

"Tabby said that dinner's ready," said Tad as he picked up Reesa.

Lexi hugged Tad.

"Thank you, sweetie…Shall we?" Lexi asked as she took Houston's arm. Houston led his family to the dining room.

Lexi and Houston stood together to greet their first guest of the evening. Raymond opened the door to Appel. She stepped in, took off her coat, and handed it to Raymond.

"Hi Raymond! Looking good," Appel said with a teasing tone.

"Thank you, Miss Appel. Might I say you look very lovely tonight?" Raymond said with a smile.

"Appel, you look beautiful," Lexi said and gave her a quick hug.

"Yes, what a lovely gown," Houston said as he gave her a hug.

Appel had on a dark blue crushed velvet gown with a v-neck. The gown had a golden rope belt at the waist that matched the delicate thin golden rope necklace she wore.

"Thanks! I got it from my grandmother, believe it or not! She said it showed off my hair," Appel said as she patted her curls.

"It does! And beautifully so," said Tabby as she stopped on her way to the great room. "Will ya be stayin' the night?"

Appel was a frequent visitor and even had her own room for times when their Bible studies ran into the wee hours.

"Yes, I don't like the cold, and there were flakes here and there. I don't do snow," Appel said wrinkling her nose in distaste.

"Snow? I hope Jeff and Dotty make it okay," Lexi said, peering out the door's side window.

"It's just a few flakes, but you know me," Appel said as she put her hand to her mouth and giggled.

They walked into the great room. The children were sitting on the floor listening intently as Reeve's told them a Christmas story.

"Wow, you guys sure know how to do Christmas. I'm totally in the Christmas spirit now," Appel said as she looked the room over.

"It's my favorite time of year," said Lexi as she led Appel to the sofa by the fireplace.

The door bell sounded, and Lexi's heart jumped. She looked quickly at Houston, and he took her hand and winked at her. They had not seen Dotty or Jeff since before they had gotten married. Lexi wasn't sure of either of their reaction to coming into their world. She knew that they had gotten married a few months ago, but that was the only news she had gotten.

Houston squeezed her hand and smile. Lexi sighed, and they went out to greet their guests.

Raymond was taking their coats, and Dotty was making sure her shoes were not wet as Lexi and Houston approached.

"Jeff! Dotty! So happy you made it," said Houston with a grin as he kissed Dotty's cheek and shook Jeff's hand.

Lexi gave Dotty a quick hug and then looked at Jeff hesitantly.

"Good of you to invite us Houston," Jeff said and then turned to Lexi. "Little Lexi, as beautiful as ever," he said then took her hand and kissed it.

Lexi peeked at Dotty and let out a breath when she saw Dotty smiling.

"Appel said it was starting to snow. I hope it wasn't a problem getting here," Lexi said with a small smile.

"Not at all," said Dotty. "There's not much coming down at this point. Even if there was, we wouldn't have missed this for the world!"

Dotty and Jeff look at each other and each let out a small giggle.

Lexi stiffened. Her heart beat so fast her face began to flush.

"Let me explain," Dotty said quickly, seeing Lexi's discomfort. "Jeff and I have gone through some life changing events that, while painful, they have brought us together. We're not those same selfish, spoiled brats we were." Dotty took Lexi's hands and asked "Lexi, can you ever forgive me for the way I treated you?"

"Of course! I was just as selfish and probably even more spoiled." Lexi laughed as she hugged Dotty tightly. When she leaned back to look into Dotty's eyes, she saw tears and realized her own eyes were watering.

"And I was a real jerk the last time I saw you both. I humbly beg your forgiveness," Jeff said so sincerely Lexi reached over and hugged him also.

Jeff turned and hugged Houston then planted a long kiss on his cheek which made everyone laugh. "My friend, we have catching up to do. Dotty and I will tell you our story later, but the end result is that we have become Christians."

Lexi's hands flew to her mouth as she gasped. "Jeff! Dotty! How wonderful!"

Dotty's smile lit up her eyes which still had tears in them.

"Dotty? Are you Okay," Houston said taking her arm.

Dotty looked at Jeff who nodded as he put his arms around her. "Jeff and I are going to have a baby!"

"That's wonderful! Children are so amazing," Lexi said hugging Dotty again.

"Let's go into the great room. You can meet our four," Houston said as he moved his eyebrows up and down.

"Four? You've been busy," Jeff laughed and put his hand on Houston's arm.

"We have a house full of love," Houston said then pointed up at the mistletoe. They all laughed and both couples kissed.